BI-yker Vixen

A Nonfiction Memoir
By Dr. April A. Jones

The story has been embellished.

BI-yker Vixen
More Than I Should

A Nonfiction Memoir
By Dr. April A. Jones

Sankofa Publishing 2024
All rights reserved. Published in the United States by Dr. April A.
Jones, a division of Sankofa Achievement Center, Inc. Nashville,
Tennessee.

www.thesac.org
Library of Congress Cataloging-Publication Data
Names: Dr. April A. Jones, Author.
Title: BI-yker Vixen.
Identifiers ISBN- Print 978-1-7379930-5-6
Audio 978-1-7379930-6-3

Jacket Illustration Dr. April A. Jones
Editor I: Dr. April A. Jones
Editor II: Kanisha N. Sizemore

Manufactured in the United States of America

Dedications

This book is dedicated to everyone who has helped me on my journey of motorcycling. This is from learning how to ride long distance to becoming an independent rider and learning the protocol of motorcycling and crossing state lines.

This book is dedicated to all of my veteran women motorcyclist across the nation who have inspired me to become more and do more with my motorcycling platform.

Throughout my journey, I have met incredible people who have shared their knowledge and passion for motorcycling with me. From the experienced riders who took me under their wing and showed me the ropes, to the kind strangers who stopped to help me when my bike broke down on the side of the road, I am grateful for each and every person who has helped me along the way.

As a woman in the world of motorcycling, I have faced my fair share of challenges and obstacles. But through it all, I have been inspired by the strong and fearless veteran women motorcyclists who have blazed the trail before me. Their courage and determination have shown me that anything is possible if you set your mind to it.

I hope that this book will serve as a source of inspiration and guidance for anyone who is embarking on their own journey of motorcycling. Whether you are a seasoned rider or just starting out, there is always something new to learn and discover on the open road. So let's rev our engines and hit the pavement, together.

Dr. April A. Jones

TABLE OF CONTENTS

The new tire I had just got, flat , "Damn!" I cursed out loud, "So much for a nice ride down to New Orleans" There I was stuck on the side of the interstate staring at a skinny ass busted tire, not going nowhere. The weight of the pistol in my pocket eased my mind some as I look around and place my helmet on the ground to signal my distress. Taking out my phone I think to myself, "At least the sky is blue and I got AAA."

Before she passed, Momma always told me "Everything happens for a reason." Three hours later, after watching the tow truck haul my bike away on the trailer, I called an Uber to take me to 5319 Getwell Ave. I made sure to tip the kind driver before exiting the vehicle so I wouldn't forget. Obliged to do so, grateful that he got me off that busy interstate where the tow truck driver deserted me on twos, two feet that is.

My first place of business after spending three hundred on my 21" front tire, now a fucking Uber, tow, room cancellation charges and other racked up unnecessary money was getting revenge. Somebody was going to pay! This mother fucker had one job to do and that was give me a new non-defective tire. The garage building where I bought the tire from is a tire shop and a mechanic shop that I enter swiftly with my helmet in my hand. It's a small tire shop and there isn't much room upon entry just a front desk, which was empty and two chairs for customers to sit and wait.

I walked past the desk with my eyes searching for the guy that just put my tire on the bike two days ago. I see him bending over looking at another bike's rear tire, just then he stands up and asked me how he could help me. In one motion I pulled open my defense stick and commenced to whopping his ass! I whaled on his ass for at least two minutes to account for my fucked up tire. As I walked away folding my stick up, he lay on the ground bloody, moaning in pain.

My name is Remy, I have two grown children, an ex-husband and a girlfriend. Most people call me doctor Remy because I earned my doctorate degree in educational leadership from Tennessee State University. My hometown is Chicago, but I have raised my children in Nashville for the past 14 years since my honorable discharge from the United States Army. I have gotten in some trouble throughout my years, but one thing for sure, I don't take no shit!

Present Day, 2012

Rolling over in the bed listening to the light sleet hitting my window, I peer at the clock. It's three am in the morning. It's dark outside with a thin coat of snow on the ground. I bet my students are excited I think to myself. I teach at a predominantly Hispanic elementary school in Nashville and my second graders love the snow, I on the other hand love the snow days. I mean in Chicago where I am originally from, we would be walking in 4 or more inches of snow to school, I mean there just wasn't any such thing of school closings due to the snow, but here in Nashville just a little bit of some snow and the city was shutting down. Just then, my phone rings, hello: This is Metro Nashville Public Schools calling with a weather update, all schools are closed today. There will be no before or afterschool care. Message repeating, This is Nashville," click! I hang up the phone with the biggest smile on my face. As I twinkle my toes underneath the blanket, I wonder what will I do today, but for now I close my eyes and drift back to sleep.

The sun woke me up shining through my window. As I peered through my blinds out the window I noticed the ground was nearly dry, children in the neighborhood were playing and the snow day has turned into a great day. I walked to my garage where my new motorcycle had been parked while awaiting my Riders Edge course from Harley Davidson.

My guy friend Durk, after riding my bike home for me after I purchased it, told me to leave the bike alone until I took my class, but I have been secretly riding up and down the street after work practicing on my own. I only slid, fell and picked the bike up out of the mud once, oh and I fell over on three parked cars in the past few weeks, but I think I got the basics.

I picked up my phone to call my homegirl Mona. I knew she would be out riding with her crew on this beautiful day. When Mona answered the phone she was laughing and I heard the guys laughing in the background talking shit as usual. "Hey Remy," She said. "Hey Mona where y'all at," I asked her. Mona said they were down by the lake hanging out on their bikes. I told them "I would be right there." Mona said "ok, drive safe and hang out with us until we pull back out." She didn't know I was not about to drive anywhere. Today was the day that I was going to take the bike out past the block and around the corner. I laced my sexy black boots up and slid them, my jacket and helmet on. I was so excited my palms were sweating inside my gloves, my helmet was fogged up and my glasses kept sliding off my face.

As I pulled out of my garage slowly, I looked both ways and preceeded with caution. By the time I reached the third stop light you couldn't tell me nothing. Fifteen minutes later I was pulling into the park and I spotted the crew over by the water. I rode over slowly and shocked the shit out of all of them! In between the clapping and cheering for me, one of the brothers told me to turn around and park next to them.

I slowly head down the boat ramp with the intentions of turning around and it was at the moment I realized I didn't know what the fuck I was really doing and was about to ride clear into the water. I forgot where the brake was and gave it throttle. Mona was killing herself laughing as the guys ran to save me from riding off into the water.

We hung out at the lake for about thirty minutes. As my so

called friends continued cracking jokes about the look on my face as my bike headed down the boat ramp. I have to admit, I was embarrassed, but it was funny indeed. I peered at the sky and noticed the clouds were quickly moving in our direction. The cumulus clouds were dark grey and swiftly approaching us from the distance. "Hey Mona, look at the sky! We need to get rolling," I said. We all agreed to mount up and head home.

I rode home, taking the streets cautiously. As I sat at the red light, the car next to me rolled the window down and the driver yelled at me, "hey you looking good on that bike girl, but you better hurry up and get home. It is already storming on the west side." I nodded, smiled and said "thank you." As soon as the light turned green, I hit one down and two up. I was literally three minutes from my house when the sky bottomed out on my head.

I could not see in front of me. I was beyond nervous. I took my time and made it home safe and soaked. When I took my boots off, I poured about one cup of water out of them. I begin laughing to myself thinking how dangerously fun, I thought that was. I couldn't do anything but shake my head as I let the garage door shut.

Two weeks later, my riders course was here. My friend Jasmine and I took the class together. We met registering for the class and decided to take the class together. During the class she fell off her training bike. I was around on the other side of the course when I noticed her get thrown off and into the fence face first. I continued to ride across the lot and parked my bike as fast as I could to assist. Her head was bleeding when I ran over to her side. I told her it was going to be ok. I could here the instructor calling 911 requesting an ambulance.

 The ambulance arrived fairly quickly and carried her off to the hospital. I followed her in my car. She needed several stitches and she said she was done with trying to learn how to ride a motorcycle. She said, "I thought I had it, then I lost control. That was too scary and I never want to be scared like that again." I was shaken up as well from seeing the accident, but I know for sure I wasn't going to give up and not get my motorcycle license. I mean I know its dangerous, but I just felt like I was built for this. The next week I returned to finish my Riders Edge course. "I see you know how to ride your bike, now I'm going to teach you how to save your life," Mike the instructor says to me as I completed my figure eights around the course easily. I passed my class and was officially ready to hit the road.

Back at home staring at myself in the mirror thinking to myself, "I'm a biker chick!" 5 feet 10 inches, chocolate complexion with a few smooth moles starting to appear on my face. My Afro is naturally beautiful and it is huge. I didn't think about all this hair being under a helmet when I went purchasing my motorcycle, but I'm going to figure it out. I need to find me some leather chaps to cover up my thighs and hips. I fell asleep daydreaming about my fashion and the look I wanted to have while out on my bike.

"Girl wake your ass up! All you do is take naps," Mona said as she woke me up. I knew I shouldn't have answered the phone. "What's up girl? What do you want? It's 7 o'clock on a Saturday morning!" I replied. Mona yells into the phone again, "wake your ass up!" It's a motorcycle day party and then they having a party later tonight at the Grand Ball Room and I want us to ride through. I couldn't help but to look at the time one more time to make sure I wasn't tripping. Like is she really calling me this early. "Hello, is anyone there?" She demanded. I rolled my eyes and responded, "yes girl I will be ready, now I'm going back to sleep." As I hung up the phone, all I could think about was what I was going to wear.

Around one o'clock I was all ready to go. I put my navy polo jeans on because they fit me a little snug and I wanted to show off my curves for sure. I had on my long sleeve polo shirt and some polo boots, baby you can't tell me I'm not fine today. I could hear Mona's 1400 Busa pulling up all the way down the street. She loves revving up the throttle even when she just sitting still. I open up my garage, lock down my house and was ready to ride. "Don"t forget your gloves Remy," Mona yelled from up under her helmet. I already had them in my back pocket, so I whipped them out and waved them in the air so she could see I had them. As I mounted my bike, I pulled out onto the street and Mona led the way.

It was sunny, the clouds were fluffy and the birds were happy in the sky. I was happy too. I'm looking to my left and looking to my right feeling real comfortable now on my cruiser. We pulled up to a motorcycle clubhouse and not only could I smell the food, I could see the smoke coming from the big ass grill. The music was loud and banging playing some line dancing music. Some of the ladies were getting it started on the dance with cups in their hands.

As soon as I put my kickstand down in the gravel, I had three guys already walking towards me to offer a hand in helping me park in that gravel. I'm thinking to myself as they approach, I needed some help parking in the gravel, but for damn sure I wasn't about to let them know. What I look like having the guys help me park my own bike. "You good sis, Rod Boy asked." Rod Boy was fine as hell. He is the Vice President of Slam Ryduz Motorcycle Club. He is tall, about 6'4" with a big beard hanging from his face. Chocolate and muscular and as I heard from the streets talking, he has a way with the ladies and plenty of money. I hugged him and thanked him for asking, but I told him I was good. As I released him, I was thinking that he smelled good too.

Meanwhile Mona was standing back looking at me shaking her head. "What girl I asked her, and she just parades on past me saying, "nothing" and smiling. I followed her on into the clubhouse. The ladies are dancing, they all had on different colored vests. I asked Mona why some of the ladies had on pink or red, even blue vests and then it was maybe two ladies who had on Black vests. "The ladies in the colored vests are in a social club, the ladies that have a black vests on like the guys wear are riders in motorcycle clubs." She explained to me. You can only wear or rock a black vest if you ride on twos," Mona says. My head is already like, ok I need to get me a black vest and I need to join a club. I'm digging "The Set" as Mona called it. Just then while I'm standing and watching the ladies dance, Rod Boy walks up to me and asked, do you want something to eat or drink?" "Thank you, and yes I will take both," I responded. I followed him to the bar, he asked me, what do you want to drink Remy?" I told him, "I'll take a beer and a fish sandwich." I told him. I really wanted some Remy VSOP, but I was on my bike. Rod Boy asked me while waiting for the drinks, "how long you been riding."

I told him, "I am a newbie and only been riding for a little over a month." He said, "well looks like you doing good, I can take you out riding around the back roads to help you get some more practice." He handed me his phone and told me to, "put your number in my phone." I'm thinking to myself, yeah this is a setup. I gave him my number though, I couldn't even say no. He exuded my attention.

All of a sudden as we're standing there, Mona comes running inside the clubhouse along with about 10 other people.

Rod Boy, they out here arguing bro and they talking about pulling out pistols!" somebody shouted. Rod Boy told me to stay inside and he ran outside promptly. Mona said, "we can't never have a good time without some drama popping off!" Outside it was getting heated, Rod Boy was in between two of his members and another guy. Apparently this guy doesn't know Set protocol and about to get stumped to the ground.

The two members told Rod Boy that this guy was being disrespectful to their clubhouse which is a big no. The problem really boiled down to the guy was drunk and touched on one of the lady women in the club inappropriately. The two club members told him he had to leave and the guy got defensive and said fuck this club and them hoes. The police pulled up and Rod Boy spoke intelligently to the officers about the situation. He told the officers that he had deescalated the guys and everyone was about to go home because the party is over.

The officers knew Rod Boy and they respecting him and his club, Slam Ryduz as valuable members of our community. The officers turned around and made their way back to the squad car pulling off without a care in the world of this situation. Rod Boy was so sexy to me the way he talked to everyone involved. As he was standing and telling his club members to meet up at a certain time for their annual party, I couldn't keep my eyes off of him. He looked like he was in serious conversation, so I decided to take my eyes off of him just in time to notice Mona staring at me waiting for my response to what she apparently had just said to me.

"Remy, Mona repeated herself, "girl lets go and get ready for tonight." We walked to our bikes mounted up and rode home. When we got to the fork in the road where we went our separate ways we both threw up the peace sign. Mona hauled ass on her Busa, while I considered living on the dangerous side doing 80 on my Sportster 883 she was probably at 110 miles per hour. When I was one exit away from my house, I even turned it up a notch and went 85 mph!

My daughter and son were away for the summer with their father. We separated and divorced a few years ago, but I made sure to keep their relationship secured. Not only does it take a village to raise a child, but I didn't have a father figure around while I was growing up so I wanted make for damn sure mine had different than what I had. I called them on FaceTime before heading out for the evening to check on them. We laughed and chatted for maybe fifteen minutes before it was time for them to get ready for bed. "Good night you two and I love you both," I said. "You too mom, my daughter cheerfully said." "Ride safe mommy, my son said."

Tonight I decided to black myself out. I put on some black leather pants, a black laced blouse that showed the top of my breast quite nicely. I put my black Harley Davidson boots on with some slouchy black HD socks that you can see from the top of the boot. My hair was braided down to the back, then I wrapped a rhinestone studded Harley bandanna around my head. My makeup was flawless. "Shit, I look so good I might just fuck myself tonight," I told the mirror mirror on the wall. I decided to take the edge off and smoke me a little weed and work on my research paper for school while I was waiting for Mona to let me know she was ready. I attend the local university and I am working on my Masters degree in educational leadership. Education is one of my foundational core values. My mother made sure of it when she would whoop me if my grades dropped below a 'B.'

"The party is jumping I can't even lie. Slam Ryduz MC knows how to throw a party," I told Rod Boy in my Felicia from Friday voice. He shook his head and told me to let him know if I needed anything. "Ok Mr. VP, I said as I walked away making sure to turn slowly so he can see all of these long legs walking away carrying all ass. Mona was on the dance floor getting her groove on. I decided I wanted to do my little two step as well, so I headed to the dance floor. Mona and I danced, gave each other high fives and giggled all night long. I mean it was midnight before I knew it.

All of the clubs a had gathered around in groups and begin walking in line dancing and repping their clubs one by one. "Mona, what are they doing," I asked. "This is called the color count. All of the clubs are walking through and they count how many vested members are in attendance for the night and the club with the most members receive a trophy. The largest club from out of town, the rider who rode the longest to be here and other awards are given out at this time." Mona concluded as she sipped on her drink. I am amazed at the fellowshipping of brothers and sisters, I was thinking. I am more thinking about joining one of these clubs. I'll just keep hanging around and watching. Surely I can find a home in one of these clubs.

When the lights came on, I could tell that many people had left already. Mona was standing by the bar and waved for me to come on so we could leave. Just as I was walking out the door about to open it, Rod Boy, Mr. VP himself grabbed the door handle and opened it for me. I looked at him, smiled and said "thank you." That night, Mona and I rode off and the night was clear. It was one beautiful windless night. We took the back roads and I couldn't believe the freedom I felt while riding on two wheels.

It is the end of the summer, my kiddos are coming back home. I had been riding most of the summer independently back and forth to my classes for my Masters in curriculum and instruction. I was preparing to get back to teaching a third year with my second graders at the local elementary school. We had back to back meetings preparing for the new policies and plan for the new academic year. I typically jumped on the bike and rode to the professional development building where teachers have workshops and breakout sessions. I have a pretty busy life, but I was determined to finish everything I started.

Chapter Two
Black Calvary

"Momma! I can't believe you made it down from Chicago to be here, I am so excited." I told my mother as I hugged her. "You know I wasn't going to miss it." My mother replied. She told me she bought me a black mini pencil skirt, some black pumps, a waist high black blazer and some black feathered earrings. "Um that's a no for me on the feather earrings, I said." My mother laughed as she turned around to open this big box. "And for the grand finale, when you put this on I want yo ass to stomp across that stage!" She pulls out this big ass black floppy hat. My eyes rolled in the back of my head, but I had to admit, it was elegant.

My children, my mother and I loaded up into the car and went to my graduation ceremony. I am the first one in my immediate family to not only receive my Bachelor's degree, but my Master's as well. My mother always preached to me that no one can take my education away from me. This has been my motivation since I was in elementary school, scared to bring home a 'C' because I didn't want her to beat my ass. The ceremony ended just as slow as it started. As they called the doctoral recipients first, I pledged to be up front siting in the front row next time receiving my Doctoral degree.

I wanted to be one of the first to be called up to get my degree, maybe that way I could sneak out of the building after I walk across the stage. I mean don't get me wrong, I am proud of everyone who are in these seats and waiting their turn to be called up to receive their degree, but why lord does the ceremony have to take so long? I think it should be a side door and as soon as you walk across the stage, take your picture with the President of the University, we should be directed right down the steps of the stage out the mother fucking door into the parking lot.

That afternoon, Mona and I decided to go out to the Set party to celebrate my achievements. We met up at our regular gas station to fill up the bike tanks, grab some cash from the atm machine so we could support the club and then we headed out. Mona signaled for me to pull up next to her at the stop light so we could pose and take a selfie picture. She is a Facebook and social media junkie. I'm still mad that every time I get the hang of one social media platform, here comes another that I have to learn. I leave it up to her though.

We made it safely to the club and the first person I spot is Rod Boy. He came to give me a hug and talk somewhat. "I see you still ain't went to trade your little motorcycle in yet, huh Remy?" "Now why would I do that Mr. VP?" I candidly responded. "I just thought you were ready for some speed, ready to get off that old lady Harley," as he laughs like that shit was funny. "No I love my Sportster thank you very much!" I chuckled at him.

As we entered the clubhouse, I heard Rod Boy behind me very

closely in my ear say, "oh yeah by the way, congratulations Remy."
"Thank you, I replied." "Drinks on me," he goes further to say.
"I'll have a Remy VSOP on the rocks and a Michelob Ultra and
thank you again seriously," I said. Mona followed me to the bar
and said " Yeah Rod Boy, I'll have a Jack and coke too," laughing
like, where mine at negro!

I partied all night long and met some cool people. It had been
almost two years since I had learned to ride my bike. I still wasn't
in a club, but I was still looking. It just seems like the comradery is
what I'm missing while I'm out here riding back and forth to work
and around town alone. For tonight though, I'm just chilling and
still peeping out the scene of the different clubs. The women seem
slightly clicked up, but that is to be assumed I guess because they
have the same center patches on their backs, right?

It had been about two months. I was back in school pursuing
my Doctorate degree. I now teach high school, my children are
growing up wonderfully. I hate when I have to discipline them, but
I know if they don't get the discipline at home someone in the
streets will give it to them. Everything was all good in my life. I had
just finished putting my dishes up from cooking and having dinner
with my two littles when my phone rang. "Ring, ring, ring!" "Ring,
ring, ring!" I looked at the caller ID and it was my mom.

"Hey April, what you doing?" she asked. "Hey momma, I'm
getting ready for bed, I just finished putting the kiddos to bed and

cleaning up my mess I made in the kitchen," I replied. She sounded winded on the phone. "Are you ok Ma?" I asked her curiously." I don't know April, I'm not feeling well, can you come take me to the hospital?" she said. My reply was plain, "of course, I can." I called into the substitute phone line to request a sub for my classroom. I made sure my lesson plans were together, prepared for my 7 hour road trip up to Chicago to help my mother.

Mona called me and woke me up out of my sleep. "For the life of me I can't understand why you don't call me during normal business hours," I grumpily said. She says, "My bad, but I just wanted to let you know I am going to a motorcycle club meeting to find out about joining them and I want you to come with me." I popped my eyes open a little wider as she was speaking about an interesting topic in the middle of the damn night, "what's the name of the club," I asked Mona. She said, "it's called the BCMC Black Calvary Motorcycle Club, it's a coed club based upon the rich history of Black military soldiers who fought in the civil war as free slaves and I will tell you more tomorrow!" I told her I was going to see about my mother in the morning, but when I get back we can talk more because I was very interested. "Goodnight Remy, and I pray for your mom and safe travels for you." "Goodnight Mona and thank you."

The next morning I woke up early. I hated to pull my children out of school for the day, but I didn't have an alternate hand in the matter. The life of a single parent. We rode up singing and dancing together, but I couldn't get the phone call from Mona out of my head. I was really very interested. "Ring, ring, ring," I turn the music down. My mother is calling me "hey April where are yall at?" she asks. I looked around at the signs and checked my GPS, "we are just passing Indianapolis, see you in about three more hours."

It was time to stop one last time to get some gas. The children and I loaded up on a few more snacks, took our bathroom breaks and just as we were walking out of the door of the Pilot gas station a few bikers were pulling in. I immediately stared to find out what their center patches read. "I'll be damned," I said. My son looked up at me surprised, "what's the matter mommy." Laughingly, I replied "there goes some of my new club members!" Of course he had no idea what I was talking about, neither did I for that matter.

We made it back to the car and upon driving I started thinking about my mom. My mother uses a walker to get around. She is recently retired from her medical career as a nurse for over 30 years, overweight and terrified of going to the doctor. She told me of a story one time when she was sexually assaulted while seeing a doctor when she was a much younger woman. That experience, along with gaining weight over the years, dealing with physicians and medical staff who are racist against obese women; especially black obese women, had made my mother hate going to the doctor. She felt that she could self medicate and treat, unless it was dire. I knew it was dire when she called me and asked me to come from Nashville to take her to the doctor.

When we made it to the clinic I was so happy that I got my mother out of the house and to the doctor so we could find out what was wrong with her, aside from the lymphedema in her legs. The nurse came to get us from the waiting area and takes my mother to the back. I stayed in the waiting area with my children. I began researching a little history about the Black Calvary Soldiers MC while I waited for my mom. Upon my research I began reading and I learned that the Black Calvary had a proud military legacy.

The remarkable courage demonstrated by these proud African American soldiers in the face of fierce combat, extreme discrimination in the Army, deadly violence from civilians and repressive Jim Crow laws continues to inspire us today. In 1866, an Act of Congress led to the formation of six-all Black peacetime regiments, later consolidated into four regiments that developed the name Black Calvary. The main duty of the Black Calvary during this time was to support the nation's westward expansion by protecting settlers, building roads and other infrastructure, and guarding U.S. mail.

Much attention was given to the irony of African-American soldiers fighting native people on behalf of a government that accepted neither group as equals. I thought back to the hardship I faced while I served my time in the Army, I thought about racism in America and my ancestors in their quest for equality. "This is the perfect club for me," I mumbled to myself as to not sound crazy like I was talking to myself.

My mother comes from the back and proceeded straight towards the elevator. She can't walk very fast, but she damn sure was trying. As the elevator closed us in I noticed tears falling from my mother's eyes. My mother isn't a crier at all. She is tough, raised by her grandmother because her mother passed away when she was twelve years old. She dropped out of high school because she was pregnant then later returned to school to not only attain her general diploma, but she continued on to get her nursing license. She walked three miles from home to school and back every day to complete nursing school.

I have always seen my mother tell somebody where they can kiss her black ass. Her saying has always been "I'm fat and I'm going to always be fat, but I bet you can't kick my ass!" To see her in that vulnerable state as we descended to the first floor of the clinic my heart ached for my mother. My vixen kicked in and before I knew it I was headed back up to the doctor's office.

I thought to myself as I stepped off the elevator, here we go! "Ma'am excuse me can I help you?" the first nurse asked. I ignored her and kept walking right past her around the nursing station desk, down the hall looking left and right inside the different offices. Nurse number two yells, "call security!" I ignored her ass as well. I finally found the doctor who had just spoken with my mother. Her eyes were big as I stepped into her office and stood right in front of her desk. I looked her up and down, "my mother Deborah Jones was just in here, I don't know where you got your fucking degree from or how you practice medicine, but I just drove almost eight hours to bring my mother to see you so you can help her. This is a person who doesn't enjoy doctors visits already and you just proved why. You need to get a better handle on how you speak to patients and learn some better bedside fucking manners, maybe even some damn compassion. She stood up, "get out of my office, now!" As security was getting off one elevator, I was entering the other side. My mother never did tell me what happened in that room.

When I returned back home to Nashville, a week later my mother called me to alert me the doctor's office sent her a certified letter in the mail stating that I could no longer enter the premises of the clinic ever again. I told my mother we were finding her a new doctor. She actually thought this shit was funny. After hearing her laugh over the phone, hell I started laughing too. We laughed for like ten minutes. I guess it was funny how I got myself kicked out of a doctors office. I chuckled all the way to sleep. Deep down I think my mom was proud of me for standing up for her.

It was the day I had been waiting for. Mona and I were going to sit in on the Black Calvary monthly meeting. The executive board met first while Mona and I sat in the lobby with the general members of the club. After the excutive members met, they opened up the door for us all to enter. The board members conducted roll call, gave the treasurer's report regarding the club's transactions and bank account. I thought to myself this is so well organized.

The secretary was writing down and recording the meeting minutes. They discussed old and new business of the club. The new business was about the next charity event and donation they were going to give to the charity. Mona and I were new business as well. The Sergeant At Arms asked Mona to step out while they interviewed me first. When Mona stepped out, the club members began drilling me with questions. "How long have you been riding? Do you own a motorcycle and what size is it? Why are you interested in joining the Black Calvary? Do you have children? Are you married? What do you do for a living?"

Shit, I thought to myself as I began being honest with all of the members who sat quietly and attentively awaiting my response. "I am a United States Army Veteran, I am a single mother of two. I have a daughter and a son who I love dearly. I served in Afghanistan and upon returning home, I began my educational journey to become a Doctor of Leadership. I currently teach high school math, I own a Harley Davidson Sportster 883 and I have been riding for a year now. I am interested in learning more and possibly proving that I have what it takes to be a valuable asset to this organization. I am in awe of the hardships the men of the 9th and 10th Regiment Black Calvary soldiers overcame. I believe in the mission of this organization. I started my own nonprofit organization working with children so I can appreciate the charity component of this organization as well. Thank you for allowing me time to speak and join your meeting today."

As I stood there looking around, I could see the smiles starting to appear on their faces. The Road Captain yells out, "Oh I like her already, but she going to have to get off that little ass Sportster!" They all began laughing. The President told me that they had all of my contact information and would be in touch after they discussed it as a club. He stood up and said, "this is a riding club, we have chapters all across the nation which means we ride. It also means that this is an expensive club. Your affairs need to be in order to be a member of this club especially as a single mother. Thank you again for your interest and please send your friend in as you step out."

I pointed to Mona and told her it was her turn. She looks at me and ask, "how did it go?" I told her "it was cool, you got this!" Mona was in there for about twenty minutes before she walked out of the conference room. She was smiling, "I want to join, she said." I looked at Mona and whispered "me too!" We walked out of the clubhouse, mounted our bikes and decided to grab something to eat before we headed home. We road to Melvin's Fish and chatted it up about the club. Mona was concerned about the expensiveness and the traveling. I was concerned with the traveling as well. I knew that where there was a will there for sure was a way.

It was two weeks later before I heard anything. I called Mona and she told me she received her offer letter to probate, "check your spam folder if you don't see it in your inbox Remy." I opened up my laptop and went straight to my Gmail. Mona was on the phone reading what her letter said. I clicked on my spam folder and there it was. As Mona read out loud I read silently listening to her, "thank you for your interest in becoming a member of the Black Calvary Motorcycle Club. At this time the club has agreed to allow you to join the club in a probation period. During this probation period you are considered a probate or a probie. If you have any questions please feel free to contact Ready, Black Calvary Vice President.

During the probation period we were required to ride fifteen hundred miles, pay all dues, participate in at least two charity events with the club and be able to recite the Black Calvary Creed verbatim in front of all the members of the club. I studied the creed daily after work. I was allowed to count my miles to and from any BCMC event. After I noticed I was stagnant at about six hundred miles, I began getting anxious and asked if I could start going to the surrounding chapters in nearby states so I can gain my miles. I was told yes, I could. Mona and I started rolling out hitting all of the nearby chapters clubhouses. We would take a picture with the President when we arrived as proof that we rode.

Six months later, Mona and I was called into a meeting and reprimanded because we completed our miles without our chapter. They decided to change the rules for incoming probates. Our miles counted, but until further notice all probates will have to wait to complete their miles with their chapter. If it takes a year, all probates will not be allowed to do what Mona and I had just hustled our asses off and done. It was time for our full patching ceremony.

This is the final requirement that needed to be fulfilled before we received our center rocker on the back of our vests. The top rocker we wear has Black Calvary and the bottom Rocker has the city our chapter is in. The center patch which we will receive has a picture of the founding member of the club wearing an old Army uniform with a sword. It was time to recite the creed and I was so nervous I was literally shaking in my boots. I stood up and confidently walked up in front of my fellow club members,

"I am a Black Calvary, and as a Black Calvary, I will uphold the standards and the traditions set forth by my chapter and the National Association of Black Calvary Soldiers and Troopers motorcycle club. I am proud of my colors and the rich history that they represent. I will wear my colors with pride and will do all within my power to educate the general public about the rich history of the 9th and 10th Black Calvary Soldiers. I respect my colors and my Black Calvary sisters and brothers. And when my riding days come to an end, I want to be remembered as one who served with dignity, a responsible biker and a Proud Black Calvary!"

I felt empowered after reciting the creed. All of my sisters and brothers congratulated me, cheered and yelled out Black Calvary! Black Calvary! I returned to my seat and joining my new club as a full patched member. Mona recited the creed, she stumbled over some of the lines. They allowed her to start over three times, but she couldn't get it out smoothly. The Sergeant At Arms stopped Mona, "Today we can't allow you in as a full patch member. You are still in your probation period. At the next monthly meeting you will have the opportunity to try again. Now go home and practice!" I hugged Mona, "oh my God, that was so intense girl I kept forgetting the next line!" She said exhaustedly. I told her, "I was nervous as fuck too!"

I wasn't worried about it, I knew Mona would get past this hurdle. Mona followed me to the embroidery shop because I wasn't going another day without my center rocker sewed on my leather vest. The seamstress behind the counter said, "I will not be able to get to this until next week, I'm sorry ma'am, but you can leave it here and come back to pick it up next week. I pulled out a fifty dollar bill and looked at the seamstress, "next week just will not cut it for me. I need this done and I need it done today. I will bring you a ton of business when you get this job completed. Here, take this bill, sew my vest up right quick and wait for more business from me from this day forth." I meant that shit sure is my name is what it is. As I walked out of the embroidery shop, Mona was snapping it up with the camera. I felt amazing.

The following month at the meeting, Mona showed up and showed out! She recited the creed and received her center patch. We were now both Black Calvary full patch members and you couldn't tell us shit! Over the next four years, I learned how to ride across the country. I learned the endurance it takes. I learned how to pray with my sisters and brothers before we mounted up on our bikes. I also learned that prejudice does exist within your club.

I had been a Black Calvary for 4 years now. My non profit organization was chosen one of the years as the charity of choice for our annual event. I prepared a PowerPoint and speech discussing why I started my non profit, the missions and values of the organization and how people could help me help our children in our communities. I began to feel as if this was my family for real. We ate together, we had Christmas holidays together, we went to church sometimes together.

I started dating a woman while in the club. I didn't know some of the wives disapproved of this lifestyle. I didn't flaunt her around, I didn't disrespect my club brothers. I brought her along to join me as my associate member. She didn't ride bikes, but because she was my significant other she was allowed to join under me. One day she and I had a domestic altercation within the privacy of our home. I was arrested and charged with a felony. Strangulation, interference with a 911 call and theft of a device over five hundred dollars. When I posted bond after that week, my club had sent me a certified letter in the mail suspending me and asking for their patches back from my vest.

I didn't receive a phone call asking if I was ok or what had happened. The By-laws code of conduct was spelled out to me in this letter. I was told that I could appeal the decision on a national level. I was so hurt. I felt alone. I felt betrayed. I never returned to the club. Mona eventually left the club as well and moved to another state. I was back as an independent rider, riding my bike and minding my business. Oh yeah, it took a whole year, but I fought those charges to the end in court and all charges were dismissed. I lost my business, my club and that nothing ass woman I was with. The one thing that I can take with me after belonging to the Black Calvary MC is that, I know how to ride my shit.

Chapter Three
MoonDance Riders

While I was sitting in my office at my non profit, I was trying to put the pieces back together from my legal woes. I was in the process of reestablishing my business with the local public school system, I got a phone call from a good friend of mine in Saint Louis. She says "I know you are upset and hurt about how your club handled your situation, but one of my mentors helped start and found a motorcycle club out of Starkville Mississippi and they have a Nashville chapter that I think you should check out, can I give him your number?" Sure, I said.

A few days later I received a phone call from her mentor named Al. Al told me that he had been watching me on social media and thinks I could help out their chapter in Nashville. He also asked if it were ok if the President of the Nashville chapter Preacher Man came by my office to give me a sort of interview and give me some history on the MoonDance Riders. My pride wouldn't let me go back to the Black Calvary so I looked forward and embraced change and a different experience in a different club.

Over the next few weeks I continued to live my life, repairing damage done to myself, my children and my organization. I was now in the process of getting my record expunged and riding my motorcycle alone. Mona was gone, I never heard from my club members again after they suspended me so basically I was solo dolo. I was ok with being alone. All I needed was my children anyway was my thinking.

It was finally time to meet the President of my potentially new club. Preacher Man was due to swing by my place around noon. I was finishing up paperwork when my cell phone rang. Preacher Man was outside, "hello dear this is Preacher Man and I'm not sure if I'm at the right place," he exclaimed. I went to go look outside to see if I saw anyone. There was this older man with grey hair standing on my porch, he looked to be about sixty-five years old. I get how he was confused because my building looks like a house. I use the bottom for business and my children and I live upstairs in the three bedroom apartment. "You must be Preacher Man," as I extended my hand out for a handshake. He smiled "and you must be the infamous Remy I have been hearing about."

After shaking hands we continued into my office where I offered him a drink or a snack which he declined both. He had a briefcase with him full of documents. He began passing me some of the papers. He says, "these are the by-laws of this club. I want you to read over them later when you have a moment." He then proceeds to tell me what he is looking for. "We don't have any members besides myself currently. I was told that you are smart, disciplined and you know how to ride your motorcycle. I would like for you to become my Vice President and help me build this chapter back up. We used to have members, but everyone left for reasons here and there. We will need to recruit and rebuild this chapter. We have dues in this club, monthly meetings and it is mandatory attend our mother chapter's in Starkville Mississippi mandatory once a year. This is a small club, we are in the process of rebuilding our Saint Louis chapter as well. Do you have any questions for me?"

I only had one question, "why MoonDance, where did the name originate from?" I asked Preacher Man. "Well, the founder and Al used to ride all night long on their motorcycles until the moon was clear in the sky. They used to stay out riding so long just enjoying the open road and traveling across the country moonlight to moonlight. They decided to form a club and call it MoonDance Riders." I thought that was pretty cool. Not a history lesson as with the Black Calvary, but I can dig some good old fashion hard work, creating a vision based on riding through the night on iron steel. "Did I answer your question," Preacher asks. As I shook my head up and down, "yes you did and that's cool!"

We sat another 15 minutes having small talk about what I did for a living and what he used to do before he retired. We decided to meet again in a week. This would give us both time to contemplate on the future of MoonDance, the Nashville chapter and Remy as the Vice President. I can't even lie, he sold me when he threw out the VP title as my position. I'm all for some leadership opportunities!

A week had passed when I called Preacher Man and told him

that I read the by-laws and I was ready to talk about my probation period, and how it works. He told me he would bring me my top and bottom rockers, that I will be on probation for 90 days and I needed to pay my dues immediately. It was a simple probation period. I was ready to pay my first payment. Preacher Man told me to get my patches sewn on and our first meeting would be in three weeks at his house. I asked if I should bring any snacks to the meeting and he advised while we were meeting there would be no eating, but after we handle club business we could eat and mingle. "I'll bring the snacks, see you soon!" I told Preacher Man.

I ran right back to the seamstress and told her to sew my new MoonDance Riders patches on the same vest I had with the BCMC. I liked the felt patches we had because that's what I was used to. Black Calvary had felt patches as well. Typically when I saw club members in majority of other clubs their patches were not felt, they were flat patches. I thought having the felt patches made us special. My seamstress did her thing as usual and finished me up the same day as I waited. I told her to keep looking for me to bring her some business because I had some embroidery ideas for a side hustle business. It's too many people I know that be looking to have embroidery work done for their clubs.

I was looking sharp with my new colors on as I rode through the town headed over to my meeting. Upon arrival I noticed a few more bikes in the driveway. Preacher Man came out as I was parking and told me to head on inside. He hugged me and held the front door open for me. From behind me Preacher Man starts introducing the other people in the room, "this is my daughter MoBetta, she will be the Secretary. This is Polo, Sergeant at Arms and this is TooTurnt, he will be our Treasurer. Everyone, this is Remy your Vice President!" Everyone of us was new and we decided to begin planning our first ride together. Preacher Man wanted us to learn each other's style of Riding. Preacher Man said we would ride down to Huntsville Alabama together for the King of the Hill Car and Bike Show. Presented by Lucky 7-11 MC/SC, the 47th Annual King of the Hill is a one-day extravaganza of hobby racing at the Alabama International Dragway. With more than 40 trophies available in multiple categories for men's and women's events.

There we will link up with our chapters from Saint Louis and Starkville Mississippi. I had never been to something like this before or even heard of it. I was excited to attend. We linked up the day of the event at an Exxon gas station. I was riding down to meet them at the gas station and just about to get off the expressway on my exit when about 8 bikes pulled up behind me. As I look in my mirror I can notice they are approaching very quickly, "what the fuck are they doing," I said under my helmet.

As they got closer I began to panic because I felt out numbered, alone and it was as if they were trying to run me off the road deliberately, but why? I slowed my bike down as we exited the expressway and at the red light as I prepared to stop, it turned green and the bikers twisted their throttles very loudly and flew past me. I must admit that was scary. They all had on black and their bikes were all black as well. They scared the shit out of me! I had a gun on me, but what was that going to do for me in that moment of being railroaded off the road.

I gathered my composure and proceeded to meet up with my club members at the Exxon. When I pulled up at the gas station the same bikers that just attempted murder on my life as I recall it were there. I put my kickstand down and unholstered my pistol. I mean if it's going down I'm going down with a fight, in a blaze! They pulled off without incident. Moments later Preacher Man pulled up, then the rest of my club members. I told them all about what had just happened to me. They asked me what colors did they have on their backs and I couldn't answer because I was to busy fearing for my life instead of observing their patches. Preacher Man told me to forget about it. We prayed together, mounted up and hit the road together in a staggered formation. I eventually relaxed and started to enjoy the day again.

The weather was beautiful. It was sunny and not a cloud in sight. I had fun riding down. I didn't have any music besides my headphones in my ear, but my Sergeant At Arms Too Turnt's bike had some loud speakers and he was blasting some old school Dr.

Dre and Snoop Dogg. I turned my music off in my headphones and jammed down the expressway vibing to his sounds. When we arrived at the drag-way, Preacher Man told us all to follow him as he led us to a tent that was set up with MoonDance Riders logo on it. The guys were fellowshipping. They had a grill going with food smelling good, the music was playing and it was truly an outdoor party. Other clubs were set up with their tents, motorcycles were everywhere.

As we approached the MoonDance tent, I began to feel nervous about meeting the other chapter members. Preacher Man hugged our National President Oh-Dawg, "Oh-Dawg this is the new Nashville Chapter of MoonDance Riders. This is Remy, Vice President." "Welcome aboard Remy," as he leaned down to hug me. Preacher Man introduced the rest of us and we all began talking and fellowshipping with our other chapters. It was a very good day.

As night began to fall, the lights were bright on the Dragway and one of the brothers from the Starkville Chapter begin prying into more about me and my history as a rider. He asked me what felt like a hundred and one questions. When he asked me what happened to my last club I couldn't believe the emotions that buried inside of me still. I was still hurt, and as I told him about my experience with the Black Calvary, I begin to tear up in my eyes. I was so embarrassed, but he put his arms around me and told me I was in good hands with MoonDance Riders.

That night we road back to Nashville together. I felt good like I had been in a therapy intervention, I chuckled to myself under my helmet. The last 30 miles I thought about all the ways I could really help build our club. I mean I was really excited for this opportunity I was about to endeavor. My first order of business was to get out and represent our clubs colors. I wanted to go support other clubs and get our name out around The Set.

I asked about the next bike night and it was at Naptown Riders clubhouse. Their clubhouse happened to be right down the street from my house every Thursday night. I rode up there about two or three Thursdays and met some people, ordered some food and a few beers. I danced and felt like I was making gains towards making an impact on The Set for MoonDance Riders.

One Thursday night as I was supporting Naptown Riders, I had two guys walk up to me and ask me to step outside the clubhouse so they could talk to me. I had just ordered a fish sandwich, a double shot of Remy and a beer. I left it on the table where I was sitting and asked one of the Naptown ladies to watch it for me. As I stepped outside I noticed everything kind of slowed down and people were basically listening in to the conversation. These two guys had on all black.

"You can't wear that vest, and I need you to give it to me now," one of the guys said. I'm looking like what the fuck are you talking about. "I'm not giving you my vest." I told him. The other guy spoke up, "You just a Probie we shouldn't be talking to you anyway, but wearing that vest is going to get you fucked up out here, who is your President?" The second guy asked me. I told him my Prez name is Preacher Man. "You need to take the vest off now or I can take it off for you! My name is Paco and you need to tell your President to give me a call ASAP. My number is (615-545-2313)." He had his hand out like I was supposed to hand over my vest. I'm not too familiar with rules and regulations, however I knew I wasn't giving my vest to some stranger. "I will call my President, you're not taking my vest, but what I will do is leave for the night," I said as I walked the fuck away.

I felt upset and hurt because none of the members of the Naptown clubhouse I was at said anything to defend me. Actually one of the ladies did call me and told me they were gone and I could come back. I'm thinking in my head, "what type of fuck shit is this, I'm supporting and spending money at your clubhouse and you let someone come and make me leave. Damn where was the support!?"

While I was driving home pissed, I called my President Preacher Man. "Hey Preach, these guys just tried to take my vest! I think it's the same guys that tried to run me off the road too. One of the guys told me to tell you to call him Asap. He said his name is Paco and he gave me his phone number." Calmly, Preacher Man says "I don't even know why you were down there, I don't hang out on the

Set and I don't follow their rules, just stay away from them from now on."

What type of punk ass shit is this. I expected him to come running and call them to tell them to leave me alone. I expected him to protect me. Little did I know my expectactions were a bit high. I let the night pass and got some sleep. The next morning Preacher Man called and said we needed to start preparing for our annual party. He said he had been hosting a party annually at a little hole in the wall club for years. He said our other chapters would be coming in to town so we needed to have everything in order.

It was the "WE" that took me out because I ended up doing everything for this annual. Preacher Man's wife became ill and was placed in Hospice one week before the party so he was really unavailable to assist. I took on the responsibility of preparing the food, the club decor, and selling raffle tickets and just being a great host. My brothers in the other chapters actually applauded my efforts. They stepped in during the party to assist me where they could. I didn't mind at all. I am truly a team player.

The party went well, we raised a little money and was in great spirits as a club until we found out we had been placed on the black list. Because we hosted a party without the consent of the board of The Set and was not officially on the Set calendar of events we were in direct violation. They basically considered what we were doing as a definite spit in the face move. I still didn't know what was going on. I wasn't educated on protocol upon entering The Set.

About a week later Preacher Man was called into a board meeting. He was fined money because apparently the party we put on was the same day as a party for another club on The Set and we basically ended up paying them a fee from our profits to even out the disrespect to the other club. If it was only one party that night, mostly everyone would have went to that one party and supported, but because we split where people had to make a choice and we were not even granted permission to host a party, we were fined and black listed.

Standing outside of the Outlaw clubhouse awaiting a meeting is scary the first time especially when you don't know protocol. The guys told us what we did wrong and told us we had to not only pay the fine, we couldn't wear our vest, only soft colors like a t-shirt with our club name on it. We were told we had to have five members, wait a year and then ask to come back before the board to confirm if we had done what we were supposed to do. This was to be done in order to be recognized on The Set as a legit motorcycle club.

My fears went away once I knew what needed to be done. Preacher Man however said we were not going to be placed in the category of all the other clubs and said we would not be following the rules. He said, "I've been doing my own thang for years and I will continue to do so!" I took that as a sign that this probably wasn't going to be the club for me. I am one who believes if we're going to do it, let's do it right. I don't like drama, I have two small children and I'm not trying to get killed over wearing a vest and some colors because I have President that don't want to abide by the rules set forth. I cut my colors off my vest and turned them in. That was the end of MoonDance riders for me, so I thought.

Chapter Four
The Set

It's been a year and I haven't really thought about motorcycle clubs. I have been riding my bike still solo around the city. I am enjoying life, still studying for my degree, raising my children and feeling great. There was one thing missing, a companion. I wanted a girlfriend or a boyfriend. I had been so busy living life that I forgot about romance and love. After the divorce between my sons father and I, I dated a few women. It had been a few mishaps with prior women I had been involved with, but I was ready to try again. I wanted a man or a woman or maybe both, shit I'm down with the poly lifestyle as well. In my spare time I would look on dating apps. I shared my profile on both the women seeking men section as well as the women seeking women sections of the app.

I began dating both sexes on the app Plenty Of Fish. I had my fun. As I'm looking through the photos of possible acquaintances there was an incoming message request from a woman that read, "I saw that you looked at my page, why haven't you spoke and when are we going to go to lunch?" Well damn that was direct, I thought to myself. She had a NP next to her name on the app. I responded to her asking what did the NP stand for and that we could go to lunch anytime! She told me it stood for Nurse Practitioner and that she was available to go to lunch the same day before she had to go clock in to the hospital she worked at. I told her to meet me at one of my little pizza joints so we could meet and chat. She agreed. I was a few minutes late arriving to the pizza spot, but she was already inside. As I walked in she didn't recognize me because the photos on my profile my hair had long locs and I recently just cut all of them off. I literally scalped my head with a pair of clippers. Sometimes in life I think we feel the need to destroy someone, something or anything when we have given our all to a cause and fall short. Relationships don't work, finances are in the dumps, the lost of a loved one, etc. I found myself in this position and the only thing I could think to destroy was my hair. I literally took out all of my frustrations on my beautiful locs and I hadn't updated any pictures on my profile. So anyway, yeah she was about to see the new Remy and I was a little nervous about it.

The restaurant is small, so I noticed her right away. As I approached her table she looked up at me with a smile as we spoke. "Hello, I apologize for being a little late, but it's nice to meet you!" "Likewise, Lyf said. I sat down and we talked for about 30 minutes as we ate. I was smitten with the conversation. I didn't think she was the most attractive woman in the world, but she was well articulated, professional and she had her life in order as far as the conversation went. By the end of the conversation we decided to continue chatting at a nearby park. "I have about another hour before I need to head to work," Lyf said. I thought about the nearest park because I indeed wanted to continue talking. I was feeling the butterflies fluttering a little bit in my stomach. "Where did you park," I asked Lyf. She said, "I'm down the block." "I will pull up and you can follow me?" I asked "Sure, let's do it!" Lyf responded.

When we made it to the park, I got out of my car and I opened her truck door for her being the gentle lady that I am. I proceeded to grab her hand and led her to the walking path, she was impressed by my confidence with me grabbing her hand and all like I've known her forever. I was excited to be with a woman who had her shit together so I was trying to impress her. She allowed me to take the lead. I think I gained a few brownie points with that move I was thinking to myself as we walked and talked more. I asked her why she called herself Lyf and she told me "it is short for Lifesaver, but I spell mine with a Y. I am in the medical field and I save lives all day long." I squeezed her hand a little more snug and told her, "that's dope!"

It was time for us to end our lunch date, but one thing was for sure on both our ends. We definitely wanted to see each other again. We did just that too. We began talking and dating and before we knew it a few months had passed when she invited me to move in with her. I didn't hesitate because I was living in a low socioeconomic neighborhood at the time and she was living in the suburban area where the great schools were. I didn't see anything wrong with moving forward to chase the opportunity of love and not to mention to move my children into a better school district.

Lyf was in a motorcycle club so I started hanging out with her and her crew. This is when I was first truly introduced to The Set. I told her what happened with the club I was in and she said "I never heard of any club called MoonDance before, while laughing hysterically at me. She really thought my motorcycle incidents were funny. After laughing though she did tell me staying in that club would've been dangerous for real if I had stayed rocking those colors like that, without permission. I knew then that I had done the right thing by getting out of the club.

Months passed and I kept riding my bike and meeting people. Club members notice me riding independently crossing state lines. I was fearless. I rode alone. I posed at the state signs grinning ear to ear feeling accomplished. I didn't realize the more I posted my riding photos the more notoriety I was beginning to get on and off The Set. It was the time of year for Bad Problems MC annual. Lyf's club was going to ride to the party and she asked me if I was going to ride and come along. "You know Bad Problems has the best party on The Set so you might want to be there!" Lyf exclaimed. I gave it about thirty seconds, "hell yeah I'm riding with y'all!" I declared.

The night of the party was beautiful. The sky was clear and it was a nice temperature. Lyf took the lead in the pack with her club. The club was all female, which I thought was the coolest shit ever. I hadn't seen or heard about an all-female motorcycle club before. Both Black Calvary and MoonDance are coed clubs. I rode next in the line up next to Lyf and the rest of the lady club members fell in after me in a staggered formation. Although I wasn't in the club, they treated me with respect and made sure I was safe. I could appreciate that. I also thought it was sweet that I was dating the president of the club.

We pulled up five deep on the bikes. The party was jumping! We could here the loud music from the parking lot. People were outside parking lot pimping, hugging, smoking, drinking and talking shit. I was in my element. The Black Calvary didn't party like this. Black Calvary MC was more sophisticated one may say. They were an older and refined group. I actually was the youngest Black Calvary in the nation during the time I was an active member. I almost won an award for it, but I had went down on my Bike in Memphis and had a bad wreck. This happened while leaving the Black Calvary Memphis Chapter's annual two months prior to the event in Eufala, Alabama.

As I was walking to the front of the stage at the BCMC event in Eufala Alabama to receive the award for the youngest member in attendance, I was stopped in my tracks because I was in my car and not on twos, so I didn't qualify for the award. They bypassed me and gave it to the young lady who was about five years older than me at the time because she had ridden her bike to the event.

I thought it was fucked up actually that I was bypassed and not given the award due to my accident. Hell they knew I had been riding with the club when I went down, being in a car shouldn't have mattered in my opinion given what the award was for.

The night was full of greatness I thought until I got rode up on in the women's bathroom. Some of the ladies in the club snorted cocaine as their recreational drug of choice. I had never endulged in that, only marijuana but this night I decided to hang with the big girls. I was snorting some coke and having a good damn time with some random female that was in the bathroom. The bathroom at this club was big enough to have a couch in it. Women were sitting around laughing and hanging out in the restroom. One of the stalls had a curtain hanging in front of it and that's where the girls and I dipped off to get high. I was seeing flashing stars in my head after about four toots. Lyf and the other ladies walked out the stall and after looking in the mirror checking their noses for any powder they began exiting the bathroom, "Come on Remy," Lyf commanded of me. I'm not in the club so I didn't have to move when they moved I thought. The random lady started asking me a few questions and asked to take a picture with me. She wasn't a biker and was fascinated with women riders. I began taking pictures with the lady and just then my phone was slapped out of my hand. I saw it slide clear across the bathroom floor. The lady looked surprised, I was stunned. I didn't know what the fuck was going on. The tension between us escalated, and it became evident that Lyf was furious as she stood, breathing heavily in my face. I didn't budge when she told me to, and I was engrossed in a conversation with another woman, earning myself a public scolding. That incident served as red flag number one, which unfortunately, I failed to heed. Embarrassed, the other ladies in the club laughed and remarked, "She told you to come on; you should've just come on, Remy!" The remainder of the night was spoiled. I no longer had any fun. My feelings were hurt, my high evaporated, and I felt like I had a bully for a mate.

The next morning, as I lay in bed with a massive headache, my cell phone chimed with a text message: "CALLING ALL RIDERS TO CHATTANOOGA, KSU 10 AM!" I didn't know who would be riding in the group, but I knew I wanted to go. It was seven in the morning, so I had time to pull my life together. I showered, prepared some Sunday breakfast for the children, and mounted up on the bike. I was determined to forget about my dreadful night at the annual gathering last night.

I put my kickstand down at the meetup location, which was in the parking lot of an old church. A couple of presidents from different clubs stood under a tree, engaged in conversation and smoking cigars. I placed my helmet on my back seat, slid my gloves into my back jean pocket, and approached the guys to introduce myself. Nervous, but relieved to see another female rider sitting on her bike, I thought, at least I wasn't the only girl. "Good morning, I'm Remy how are you all doing this fine morning!" I said as I hugged each and everyone of them. They welcomed me with warm arms. I then walked over to the lady biker and as I approached her she stood up to greet me as well, "hello I'm Remy and I love your bike!" I said as I hugged her. "I'm Peaches and thank you so much, yes girl I love my Busa," she exclaimed. She was in a club called Durby Boys MC. "How long have you been riding?" I asked Peaches. "Girl I'm old, I've been riding since I was a teenager," she said. She asked me the same and I told her that I'd been riding for about six years now. "Have you heard of Moondance Riders?" I asked Peaches. She replied that she never heard of them before. Just then, they called us all for the rides safety briefing and prayer.

We circled up in a huddle and were instructed on who the road captains would be, the distance of the ride, the mission of the ride as well as being thanked for supporting and showing up on an early Sunday morning. We held hands and prayed together. It was thirteen of us in total. Peaches and I were the only two ladies so we road in the middle of the pack together.

Riding up and down the mountains on interstate 24 from Nashville, Tennessee to Chattanooga, Tennessee is a beautiful scene, but damn I was so nervous. These fools were riding 90-100 m.p.h around these curves, had my stomach and asshole in knots! I wasn't going to let them see me sweat though. I kept the rubber on the road and pounded there and back. I felt wonderful. I met some new people on The Set and gained some respect. It was right around this time when I began being asked about joining another club.

Later that week, Lyf and her club were going to a day party to support Rebel Ryduz MC. She asked me if I wanted to ride down with them and I agreed. The Rebel Ryduz had a cool function. They raffled off some gift certificates to the attendees, grilled food and didn't charge a thing and made sure to show great hospitality. I thought this club was well put together. They didn't allow women in the club, although they did have one female rider. I was told that they shut it down for females joining some time ago. That didn't stop Dengo the President and founder of Rebel Ryduz from approaching me with a proposition.

I was standing with Tay, one of the girls in Lyf's club when Dengo walked up and put his arm around her neck. "What's up Tay, who is this?" Pointing at me. "This is Remy," she responded. "Yeah I heard you pounded down to Chattanooga last weekend, and didn't you ride to Chicago by yourself a few months ago!" He said. "Yes that was me," I bolstered proudly. He looked at Tay, "Where is your president, where is Lyfsavour?" "Lyf! Dengo want you," Tay yelled towards Lyf who was standing nearby talking to someone. When she walked over, Dengo asked her if I could ride with his crew to Saint Louis for their annual ride up the highway.

She told him, "she is not a member of my club so she can do and go wherever she wants to Dengo." He then asked me, "Remy will you ride with my club to the Lou for our Annual?" I answered matter of factly and said, "sure why not, sounds like fun." Of course when we made it home, I was asked why he asked me to ride with his club like the fuck I knew why. Red flag number two. Jealousy is a sickness. Sometimes the closest ones to you will have jealousy and all you doing is living your life. In all seriousness, I didn't know why I was being questioned by my girlfriend about riding which is what we supposed to be doing anyway, riding.

Weeks had passed, the weeks rolled into months and the months rolled over. I was still riding solo, I supported all of the motorcycle clubs when time permitted me to. I was enjoying my hobby. I have hung out with multiple clubs, I have been in several motorcycle accidents and I was still happily riding. By this time I had learned and met at least sixty percent of The Set in my area and I'm known for riding my shit.

One day Lyf asked me to join her club out of the blue. She told me that they needed another member. The number is five in order for a club to remain active on The Set and one of her members just retired. I told her, "no" just as politely as I could. Although I contiued to hang out with her club, I had no intentions on joining not just her club, but any club. Needless to say Lyf was persistent.

She approached me, pleading for assistance to prevent her club from folding due to a lack of membership. After weeks of pillow talk, I reluctantly agreed to help her and the other girls. My initiation involved completing a probationary period of five hundred miles riding with the ladies of the club. The women chose a weekend day, and we embarked on a journey, crossing several state lines surrounding Tennessee to meet my mileage quota. Despite the freezing temperatures, I enjoyed the camaraderie with the ladies. We bonded during the trip, enduring the chilly weather together. We left at daybreak, and by the time we headed back, the temperature had dropped significantly. I suggested we pull over at a Walmart to grab warmer clothes to layer up.

While passing the wine department, the idea of a good bottle of wine to warm us up struck me. Tay agreed, and we selected a bottle. Standing in the Walmart parking lot, we layered up with hoodies, hand warmers, and a bottle of wine. By the time we left that parking lot, I was pleasantly tipsy and warm. The last leg of the trip was challenging, and at some points, I doubted whether I would make it home that night. However, we all reached our destinations safely. As a result of completing the probationary period, I earned my patch and was nominated to be one of the club's officers. I proudly assumed the role of secretary for the Platinum Dymez, an all-female motorcycle club!

Chapter Five
Platinum Dymez

Our motorcycle club had a social club comprised of women who supported us wholeheartedly, despite not riding motorcycles themselves. Among them were Candy, Mysterious, TooShort, Sunshyne, and Tee. It was time for the annual Trunk or Treat event on The Set, and we were all geared up for it. Lyf brought her Yukon, which we decorated with the social club's help. We all wore costumes and contributed to the candy pile. This was my first time attending Trunk or Treat, and I was thrilled. I went to the store and stocked up on old-school candies like lemon heads, Boston baked beans, Now and Laters, sunflower seeds, Whoppers, and Sugar Daddies. Our setup was fantastic, and I brought my party speaker so we could dance, socialize, and give out candy to the kids. I was very excited!

As I was on my way, Mysterious called me through the phone, "Remy, where are you?" she asked. "I'm almost there, are you already there?" I responded. "Yes, I'm here," she said. Within thirty seconds, I parked my car. I wanted to get some extra lights to put around my party speaker, so I was running late. The children were already lining up with their bags in hand, dressed in various Halloween costumes. I quickly met up with the rest of the crew and helped with the final decorations, which included pumpkins, spider webs, and even a fog machine to create the perfect spooky ambiance. As soon as the music started playing, the kids began dancing and laughing, their happy faces lighting up as they received their candy treats. As the night progressed, more families arrived, and our candy pile started to dwindle. However, we refused to let that dampen our spirits. We continued to dance, chat, and have a great time with everyone who stopped by our setup. By the end of the night, exhaustion had set in, but our hearts were full of joy and a sense of accomplishment. The trunk-or-treat had been a tremendous success, and we were already planning for next year's event. It served as a wonderful reminder of the power of community and the joy that comes from coming together to celebrate.

Soon after, it was time for me to hit the road to Saint Louis with Dengo and Rebel Ryduz for the annual ride. When I was initially asked, I wasn't part of a club, but now I was, and it didn't feel right being the only one from my club riding out of town with another group. I raised the question at our club meeting, but unfortunately, all the SC members and my club sisters on the MC side had work commitments for the weekend of the ride. During the meeting, I sensed that either no one was asked personally to go like I had been, or they simply didn't want me to go. Despite feeling this way, I believed it would be a great opportunity to proudly fly my colors in another city, so I decided to go alone. That Saturday morning, I was all set to hit the road. My children helped me get ready, we prayed together in the garage before I departed and off I was to meetup with the Rebel Ryduz. None of my sisters in my club called to wish me well wishes or safe travels. That hurt, but I wasn't going to let that sink into my head. I needed to stay focused for this five hour road trip. I notated that red flag and put it in my back pocket for the time being. Oh yeah, I noticed Lyf didn't either and we live together. I put that notation in a separate pocket for later because that hurt was a different hurt, thats personal for sure.

My pull up game is so sweet, I was the first one at the meetup location. It wasn't long before they began piling in the gas station behind me. We hugged and greeted each other as we talked about the route and waited for the other Rebel Ryduz to arrive. I needed to use the restroom before we departed and get a fill up of gas in the bike. As I started walking towards the restroom I notice the only lady rider in Rebel Ryduz, Milla was following me into the restroom. I held the door open for her and she said "thank you, its Remy right?" "Yes and you are welcome," I told her as I let the door close.

As we stood washing our hands next to each other I hear, "I'm the hardest riding female on this Set, I don't even know why you were invited." As she sucked her teeth and walked out the door. Well damn I thought, let's skip the formalities why don't we. That too I notated and stuck in a different pocket, because the proof is in the pudding.

I adjusted my bandana, checked my smile, and casually discarded my wet paper towel into the trash, just as I was doing with all the other noise attempting to cloud my head. The ride to STL was enjoyable, and we safely reached our destination, where we were fellowshipping with the East Saint Louis Rebel Ryduz. While in the clubhouse, my phone rang. Stepping outside, I answered, "Hey, Remy, this is T-baby. I'm calling to let you know that my mom was just in a bad wreck, and we're on the way to the hospital," she said, her voice trembling with tears and heavy breathing. "T-baby, I'm in Saint Louis, but I'll be on my way now! Please keep me updated on Mona, please!" I requested. I walked over to Dengo, informing him that I had a family emergency, and that I needed to leave. "Do you need someone to go with you?" he asked, concern evident in his voice. "Can anyone ride down to Houston, Texas?" I inquired. "Girl, you're about to ride down to Houston right now!" he exclaimed. By that time, I had already input Houston into my GPS.

I departed Saint Louis, Missouri and rode straight to Houston, Texas only stopping for gas and bathroom breaks. Fueled by pure adrenaline, I had been awake for almost twenty-four hours. Though I knew I needed rest, I was determined to reach my best friend's side. The total ride took seventeen hours. Upon arriving at Baptist Hospital, I immediately checked my text messages for the latest details from Mona's daughter, T-baby. The text read:

"WE ARE IN WAITING ROOM B319; THEY JUST TOOK HER TO SURGERY."

I rushed into the hospital and pressed the elevator button, but it was taking too long. Impatient, I grabbed my helmet and headed for the stairwell. On the third floor, I scanned the area, searching for room B319 or the first person I could ask for directions. Entering B319, I found Mona's parents praying together, holding hands. Without hesitation, I joined their prayer circle. I was still unaware of what had happened or the severity of Mona's injuries, but I knew we needed urgent prayers. The atmosphere in the waiting room was charged with urgency. I allowed them to continue praying, offering comforting hugs to Mona's sixteen-year-old daughter, T-baby, holding her as if she were my own.

Exhausted, I eventually drifted off to sleep. T-baby covered me with a blanket. I was awakened by my cell phone ringing. "Mom, how is your friend?" my daughter inquired. "I'm still waiting for the doctor to provide information," I replied. "Okay, I was just checking on you," she said. As I was about to hang up, the doctor entered the room, and all of us stood up instantly. "I'm sorry to tell you that she didn't make it. We tried to stop the bleeding, but the impact of the blow to her head was too much."
The internal bleeding in her brain was too critical. I'm so sorry for your loss." the doctor explained to us.

My daughter heard the news, and told me she loved me before hanging up the phone. The screams from Mona's mother were unbearable so I had to leave out of the room. I could hear her screams down the hall, so I went outside the hospital to catch my breathe. I was hyperventilating as I walked over to my bike. I pulled out a blunt, lit it and began crying to myself thinking about my friend and all the times we had together. I went from being angry that I wasn't here with her to having feelings of joy because we had so many great times together. I puffed on my blunt until it was gone. I almost burned my fingertips.

Later at Mona's parents home, we ate dinner together. They began making arrangements for Mona and talking about the good times they had with her. We took turns telling stories of Mona's strength and courage as well as her silly wild ways that often ended up with laughter and a belly ache from the laughter. I decided to stay the week with Mona's family. The family laid her to rest seven days later. The week while I was there, I helped as much as I could trying to take the load off. I cooked, I cleaned up after everyone and ran errands as needed. I wrote a poem for the obituary to honor my friend and all of her accomplishments. The funeral was held at Greater Grant Memorial Church where her family had been members of the congregation for many years.

It was a beautiful service filled with songs and heartfelt tributes from family and friends. I couldn't help but tear up as I listened to her loved ones share their memories of Mona. She had touched so many lives in her short time on this earth, and it was evident by the number of people who came to pay their respects. After the service, we all gathered at the family's home for a repast. It was a time to celebrate Mona's life and share stories about her. The atmosphere was filled with love and laughter, and it was clear that Mona had left a lasting impact on everyone she had met.

As the week came to an end, I knew that saying goodbye to Mona's family would be difficult. They had welcomed me into their home with open arms, and I had grown to love them as my own. But I knew that Mona's spirit would live on through her family and friends, and that gave me comfort. I left with a heavy heart, but also with the knowledge that Mona's legacy would continue to inspire others for years to come.

When I returned back to Nashville, it seemed like things had changed. Lyf and I were arguing with each other often. The arguing began to fall over into the club. An emergency meeting was held where the club members told us that we could not bring the club into our personal business. Lyf yelled some profanities talking about me not being a team player and doing my own thing. I couldn't hold it in anymore. I launched to attack Lyf, but my club sisters jumped in between us. They pushed me outside the house and pushed her into a different room. I tried to calm down and act like I had some sense while I was outside pacing the grass. Lyf comes bursting out of the house, announcing that we were heading to Kentucky so Sunshyne could retrieve her bike. I thought we should probably go home and talk, but Lyf felt it was more important for Sunshyne to get her bike.

Sunshyne was in her car, and Lyf and I were on twos, following her to her house in Kentucky. She lived close to the state line, so it only took us about forty-five minutes. Upon our arrival, Lyf got off her bike and went inside with Sunshyne. Without saying anything to me, Lyf returned to her bike and put her helmet on. Sunshyne signaled that she was ready to rock and roll. Leading the way, the three of us headed back to Nashville.

About thirty minutes into the ride, we had to pull over because Sunshyne's bike was having some trouble. "It's been in the garage for about two weeks; I don't know what could be wrong with it," Sun yelled over the passing traffic. As we stood on the side of the interstate, trying to diagnose the issue with the bike, a car pulled over with its hazard lights flashing. A guy approached us, and as he got closer, I recognized him. Lyf and Sunshyne were still close to the bike.

"Podaddy, thank you for pulling over, bro!" I said as I embraced him with a hug. "No problem, Remy. I noticed your cuts and couldn't just pass by without checking if you needed help and without assisting my fellow sisters," Podaddy grunted."

He was a greasy mechanic with a big belly, his hands stayed dirty. One thing for sure though he could fix just about anything with a motor! He realized that Sunshyne only needed a new fuse. The main fuse had blown. An hour and a half had past since we first had to pull off of the interstate. While we waited for Podaddy to come back from the parts store with the fuse, I decided to bend the block to the corner store to grab a cold drink and something to roll up with. I told them I would be right back, when I returned from the store about ten minutes later no one was in sight. The bikes, Lyf and Sunshyne had left and didn't call me to let me know they had gotten back ready to ride. I rolled past slowly and then proceeded to go where I thought they would be. Thinking to myself, damn they could've told me they were about to leave.

Being in an all-female motorcycle club was becoming a bit much. The motto however was we can argue, fuss and cuss behind closed doors, but in public we should stand unified as one, as sisters. I wasn't feeling that way lately. The romance stopped in my relationship, the communication had broken down completely inside my home which in turn showed on the outside in my demeanor. Usually pretty confident of a person I am, I began feeling something in my gut that didn't feel well. Ah, I know what it is, intuition. Woman's intuition.

Lyf had came home late drunk. I sat on the couch watching her as she chatted on the phone with Sunshyne who had just dropped her off. They had been out having dinner and drinks I was told.

As she giggled and laughed while walking to the bedroom, I couldn't help but remember the early days of our relationship, where we would flirt and have meaningful conversations. But now, I was left on the couch, listening to the sound of her footsteps fading away. In the darkness, I drifted off to sleep, only to be woken by my phone buzzing at 5 o'clock in the morning. It was my mother, asking me to arrange an Uber for my disabled brother who had a doctor's appointment in Chicago. My mother uses a flip phone and can't get the Uber app so I agreed to get one ordered for my brother. My app wasn't working for some strange reason after multiple tries. With time running out, I went upstairs to ask Lyf if I could use her phone to get an Uber arranged. However, she was sound asleep, sprawled out in the middle of the bed, fully dressed. After several attempts to wake her up, I resorted to using her thumb to access her phone and arranged an Uber for my brother, ensuring he made it to his appointment on time.

As I left the bedroom, I couldn't help but feel a tinge of sadness. It seemed like we were both so busy with our own lives that we barely had time for each other anymore. I knew we needed to have a serious conversation about our relationship, but I didn't want to ruin her good sleeping. As I sat back down on the couch, I couldn't shake the feeling that something was off. Maybe it was the weird glitch with my Uber app, or maybe it was the fact that Lyf was sleeping so soundly when she's usually a light sleeper. Either way, I couldn't ignore the nagging feeling in the pit of my stomach.

But for the time being, I pushed those thoughts aside and focused on getting my brother to his appointment. I knew that I couldn't keep ignoring the issues in my own life. It was time to have that difficult conversation with Lyf and figure out where we stood. I called my mother back on the phone to let her know I had taken care of it, and his ride would be there in less than ten minutes.

"Thank you, April!" My mom says as she hangs up. My mother always told me what goes on in the dark will come to the light eventually. I began scrolling to the text message section when I knew I shouldn't. Then I thought to myself, mom also said if you go looking for shit, you going to find shit. Just then I sat Lyf's phone back down on the table. I sat there thinking about all the times I have felt like I wasn't getting answers to my questions about us in this relationship. I picked the phone back up and begin searching for a particular person who used to be in our club. She was the old president of the club but stepped down do to personal reasons. Lyf had been in a relationship with her before and they remained very close. I wondered many times were they still seeing each other and this was the morning I was going to kill the curiosity cat.

As I found the name I was looking for I sank into the couch and began reading in the dark. There was just the bright light from the cell phone beaming up the room. I could still hear Lyf snoring as I sat there violating her personal property.

I LOVE HER CHILDREN ESPECIALLY HER DAUGHTER BUT I WANT HER TO GET OUT OF MY HOUSE.

"DO YOU NEED ME TO COME GET HER OUT FOR YOU" NO, LOL I GOT THIS. I JUST DON'T WANT TO BE WITH HER ANYMORE, BUT IM TOO NICE AND I CANT PUT HER CHILDREN OUT.

"YEAH BECAUSE I WOULDN'T HESITATE!" YOU BETTER THAN ME!

"Close your mouth April." I literally just told myself to close my own damn mouth because hanging agape is what it was doing. I couldn't believe what I was reading. I continued until I had read enough for me to know that it was time to move on. However I didn't want to move on from the club. How was I going to tell Lyf that I know what she was scared to say to me. I screenshot a few of the text messages and sent them from her phone to my phone. I then texted her from my phone and said "roger that."

I placed Lyfs phone back on the bed next to her. I stood there and stared at what I once thought was a highly educated Nurse Practitioner that could teach me somethings being she was older, rode motorcycles and had her shit together. I now stare at a woman I was completely hurt and broken by. I left the room with tears in my eyes. I got dressed for work earlier than usual and headed out the door. Half way to work Lyf woke up and text me after realizing I had saw her texts in her phone. YOU ALREADY KNOW WHAT IT IS REMY! IT IS WHAT IT IS!

It was right about now when I couldn't keep the tears from falling. I had to pull my car over in a parking lot. Its like I just can't breathe! Do I need to go to the hospital I asked myself in my head as I held on to the steering wheel tightly. I miraculously made it through teaching for the day. I shut the lights off in my classroom and preceded to drive home.What normally took thirty minutes felt like forever. My heart was beating so hard as I shut the engine off of my car. I walked into the house and Lyf asked "can we talk?" I sat down on the couch and she says, "what do you want to do?" "I'm hurt and I think the best thing for me to do is to move out and get my own place. Apparently I have over stayed my welcome. Give me about thirty days to get my next move together," I responded. Lyf looks at me with a tear in her eye and says, "I love you Remy and I was thinking you could stay here and just move into one of the other bedrooms." "I will stay in the other bedroom while I'm searching for a new place, but I don't want to do the room mate thing with you, it's best I go ahead and give you your space back." I said.

I went in the bedroom gathered my clothes and placed them in the open bedroom. As I laid there quietly thinking, Lyf came into the room and laid on top of me. "I don't want you to leave, as she cried. What you read was just talk I was having with my friend. That wasn't for your eyes and you took it in a way that you can't understand because it wasn't meant for you." I held her tight and cried with her knowing I can't stay in this relationship. She slept in the room with me that night. I couldn't sleep. I stared at the ceiling.

It had been exactly 30 days when I received my email accepting me into a privately owned condominium. I was excited to move but I was optimistic that Lyf and I would remain friends maybe even work it out from a distance. I mean we were still in the same club.

Sunshyne called me the day I was moving to tell me Lyf asked her to help me move my stuff out of the house. She had a truck so I thought that was helpful. Lyf was at work, Sunshyne and I moved the last of my things from the house. While we were in the pool house, I showed her where I started painting our club colors on the walls and how I was planning to continue turning the pool house into our little club hang suite. "I've been working on turning this pool house into our little club space where we can hangout," I told Sunshyne. "I bought the paint colors and been playing around with ideas." I continued telling her as we walked around making sure I had picked up everything I was taking.

I no longer would have access to the house after today so I wanted to make sure I had everything. On the way to my new place Sunshyne says, "I'm sorry y'all didn't work out, Lyf said you drink too much and be wilding out." Stunned and embarrassed, but knowing this is my club sister and she means no harm I responded, "Yeah I'm not perfect and I'm working on myself, I don't think it was all because of that though. We had multiple issues that I really don't want to get too deep into. Let's just move forward with our club mission sis," I finalized the conversation.

Some people don't take rejection well because the moment I walked out the door Lyf decided that would be the end of my time in the club as well, little did I know. As the weeks withered on, I was forced to turn my colors in. Club meetings became unbearable, the he say she say drama was at an all time high. Our club had become a shit show and Lyf and I were the starring actresses. Lyf didn't want the club hanging out with me anymore on The Set. Shit got weird as fuck. It was me against them it seemed. I turned my colors in and continued to ride my motorcycle crossing state lines solo dolo.

CHAPTER SIX
MOON DANCE RIDERS
PART TWO

It has been two months now since I turned my colors back in to the club. I was feeling all types of fucked up. I had the love bug going on, tossing and turning at night wondering if I let the other ladies down in my club. Did I give up too easy on my relationship of three years with Lyf? Did I walk away from my commitment to the Platinum Dymez? I'm laying in the bed staring at the ceiling when Dangerous texted me the flyer for Flying Panthers MC Annual going down this weekend. Dangerous is my assistant basketball coach at the high school I work at.

We have been trying to whip these young ladies in shape, but so far the losing spree was leading the way. My girls didn't know how to dribble, pass the ball let alone shoot and actually make a shot. Dangerous played basketball in college, she rode motorcycles and I was introduced to her through Lyf. Lyf had been knowing Dangerous for years and knew that I needed major help with my basketball team. That was one of the good things she did for me while we were together. Dangerous was an independent rider and had been on The Set for many years. She was very knowledgeable of set protocol and just a good hearted person. I used to ask her why she wasn't in a club, in particularly Platinum Dymez club since she hung out with them often. She just would say, "Nah, I'm good on a club." I even asked Lyf during a conversation one time when we were on better terms about why Dangerous hadn't joined the club, she responded with, "I'm not sure what's up with Dangerous. She used to be in Assorted Chocolates with me, but she hasn't joined another club since leaving." It was left like that.

Lately, I had been feeling down and had been avoiding basketball practice and The Set. Dangerous noticed, and reached out to me, saying, "Remy, I know you and your club are going through it, but we and the girls on the team need you. I want you to also know that I don't have anything to do with whats going on with you and the girls from your club. I don't choose sides, and I am still your friend even though I knew Lyf first." Hearing this, I let my guard down and embraced the friendship we had before the drama with the Dymez. I assumed she would join the masses of the girls and follow Lyf's lead of wanting them to never associate with me anymore on or off The Set.

The club members were divided, as Lyf made it clear she didn't want them talking to or hanging out with me anymore. It felt like we were back in elementary school, with people choosing sides and spreading gossip. Feeling outnumbered, I decided to lay low for a while. However, Dangerous could sense my unease and wanted to let me know that I was not alone. I decided to give her a call to see what what's going on with the flyer she sent.

"Hey Dangerous, I haven't been out in a few weeks, so I want to go with you to the annual for Flying Panthers!" I told her as I called her back after she text me the flyer. "I need to get out of this funk," I told her. Dangerous chuckled through the phone, "yes you do Remy, lets go and have some fun, fuck all that other noise!" I told her I would meet her Friday after our basketball game and we could ride out later that evening. Flying Panthers is in Franklin, Kentucky up the road about an hour and fifteen minutes from Nashville. I dressed warm and cute for my grand reappearance with no colors on my back, once again. While I put some mascara on staring in the mirror, I wondered would people recognize me without my colors on?

The party was lit of course. I pulled into the parking lot and Dangerous followed me in her car. Dangerous had sold her bike a few years ago after she had a major surgery, so she rode other peoples bike anytime she wanted to ride. We pulled into Flying Panthers and I felt like someone had my back as Dangerous followed behind me. Even when we were on the road she made sure the cars wouldn't get behind me while I was riding. She made me feel comfortable enough to relax and really enjoy myself on the bike. When out riding and on The Set, I always feel like I need to watch my back and keep my head on swivel. Dangerous eleviated some of that stress with her keen sense of awareness and protective nature for people she is close to. I'm glad I was one of the chosen few. She plays no games and observes everything.

I put my kickstand down, took my helmet off and I couldn't believe the love I was receiving from several people that saw me pull in. "Remy! Where you been at? "What up Remy!" "Looking good girl!" The hugs and respect I was receiving had me in awe. "I told you all you have to do is ride your shit!" Dangerous nudged me smiling and said as we walked inside the clubhouse. What I learned that night, in that moment is that if you want support you have to go out and give support. Although I had been in and out of clubs, I still supported without colors on my back. I still rode my bike and minded my business. I was in the community showing support, posting photos from the different club annuals. I continued to ride my motorcycle cross state lines. I was the one who pulls up in a different city alone and walk in straight off the road hug everyone in the club, introduce my self as Remy, order me a beer and some food and fellowship. Just like that I knew some new road buddies. I knew I couldn't be shy in motorcycling if I wanted to make an impact and get my name known as a dedicated rider. I mean that was my goal at this point. It was time to use negativity from the naysayers to fuel my fire for success in motorcycling. I'm tired of being told what I can and can't do. I'm tired of putting energy into other clubs and other people. Let me see what I can do if I put all this effort into myself.

I got my own name out there and didn't know that I was doing when I was doing it, I was just being bubbly friendly Remy. Why did I let myself think that I needed colors on my back to be recognized for doing what I love to do? Standing at the bar inside of Flying Panthers clubhouse, Preacher Man begins walking towards me I can see from across the room. As he got close he hugged me tight, "Can I talk to you outside?" he whispered in my ear. "Sure, " I told him. I grabbed my drink I ordered and followed him outside into the parking lot. Preacher Man had me follow him off to the cut where it was a little quieter. "I have talked to the board of The Set, and we can get off the Black List and reestablish our club the right way here in Nashville and I need you to do it. I need to know if you have any girls that want to join. I need to know if you are willing to come back as Vice President and help me get Moon Dance Riders on the map. If you are willing, next week I want you to ride down to Mississippi so we can meet and discuss our plan with the National President." I thought about it and decided in an instant, "hell yeah, let's do it!" He hugged me again and said we would chat tomorrow. I went to go find Dangerous back inside the club.

Dangerous was already standing outside watching me from the side of the building when I walked up to the door of the club, "I was about to come looking for you" I said. "I'm always watching my surroundings and anybody thats with me you know that, I got ya back, I always know whats going on and I stay strapped and ready," she declared. "What Preacher Man wanted with you," she asked me as she calmly sipped her Michelob Ultra beer. Looking around to ensure I didn't have extra ears listening to close, "I used to be in a club called MoonDance Riders and he wants me to come back to the club and reestablish a chapter here in Nashville.

 "I remember you mentioning you were in a club before, I never heard of them," Dangerous replied still sipping her beer. "Are you sure thats what you want to do? You know you don't need no colors on your back to do what you doing." She said. "I hear you loud and clear, but I really didn't want to leave the club the first time, it had gotten too dangerous for me and I had to think about my children. Last time my Prez didn't want to abide by the protocol of The Set. This time he said we are going to do it the right way. I'm all for it and as a matter of fact are you interested in joining?" I asked Dangerous. "Nope!" She exclaimed. I laughed hysterically because she is so serious when she said she don't want to join another club. I asked her why she wouldn't join a club and was so adamant about it. "I like things done right. I don't want to be involved in any fuck shit of an organization. I sit back and watch people and how they move. I watch how they run their clubs. I shouldn't know club business yet I know just about everybody's club business thats out here right now. When my old club Assorted Chocolates stopped doing things the right way, after five years of service to them, I had to step away. I don't do mess. I haven't seen a club yet that I feel does things the right way and thats just my opinion." Dangerous said as she now was done drinking her beer and was tossing the empty bottle in the trash can.

By this time, color count was about to begin. Dangerous and I stayed and watched to see who would win the trophies for the night and enjoy the last of the D.J. I was so caught up in business most of the night I didn't get a chance to take many pictures with people like I usually do. I started my rounds saying good bye to my people I wanted to make sure to see and take some last minute photos for social media. I ran into a couple of the social club sisters from Platinum Dymez as I was finishing my final rounds and the lights came on. We hugged each other and I of course snapped a picture with my ex club sisters. Its all love, these ladies didn't do anything to me and they are very supportive. Not only did they support us as a club when I was in the club, they supported me when I needed help fundraising for my nonprofit organization I founded. I missed hanging and having good times with them I thought as I walked away.

The next day I got a call from TooShort from Platinum Dymez, one of the social club members from my old club and she told me laughing, "we got in trouble for talking to yo ass and taking that picture at the party last night, Lyf was pissed. She talking about ending the whole club! You have single handedly destroyed our club in a way Remy! Shit just ain't the same but I support you and what you are doing around The Set and with the kids in the community. Keep doing what you doing and I will continue supporting you." She said I was breaking up the club in a jokingly manner, but she was serious. She said Lyf put the word out to the members that she didn't want anyone still in the club to hang out with me, talk to me in any fashion. She also put the bug in my ear that Sunshyne had moved into the house with Lyf and rumor has it they are more than just room mates now. In her words, "Fuck them both and keep doing you Remy." I thought that was funny and so did she.

Preacher Man called me and gave me the logistics for our ride down to Mississippi. "We will meet up at eight in the morning to ride down the interstate. It will just be you and I. We are going to let the national president know that we are ready to put in the work we need to get off the black list and restart our chapter." He firmly spoke over the phone. "That's cool, and I'm ready" I replied. I was really excited this time about making some power moves around The Set in Nashville. People laughed at this club before, they never heard of the club they said. I personally have a point to prove for all of the naysayers especially the ones who blatantly doubted me.

Dangerous had been schooling me on Set protocol for months now. She told me, "in order to get support you have to give support." That word rang a bell in my head daily. She said, "it's a bunch of fucking, dick and pussy shit that goes on around The Set, but all you have to do is ride your shit, truly ride your motorcycle and your respect will come in a good way, not laying on your back for the guys or fucking for clout." I was ready, I told her that I wanted to go get it!

The meeting in Mississippi went great I thought as we rode back home. The mother chapter was in full support of us rebuilding the Nashville chapter and told us that they are just a phone call away. If we need them to come up for any club business they would come ride down on us. That's all I really needed to know, is that we had some back up if some shit popped off again like last time.

We couldn't wear our vest until we had met all of our requirements. We have four members now. We need a fifth member, and we had to wear soft colors like t-shirts until we were granted permission to wear our vests around town again. We designed some cool blue and yellow t- shirts with our names on them and for the ladies of course we added some rhinestone bling to them. We embroidered us some hoodies, hats, and scarfs with Moon Dance Riders MC all over it.

It was time to make a statement! I needed one more person to help me and I knew just who I needed. She was going to make our fifth member! I sat up on the side of my bed thinking and before I could finish my thought completely my cell phone was in my hand. "Hey Dangerous, let's go to breakfast this morning," I told her, "if you aren't doing anything and the bill is on me," I added to the tempting offer. "Oh yeah that sounds like a plan, let me get dressed!" She said. "I will come and pick you up!" I said as I pushed the end button on my cell phone. Knowing I was going to have to lay the charm on thick to get her to say she will join my club. There have been several clubs to ask her to join their clubs and she declined them all. What can I say to make this different is what I was thinking the whole ride to her house. A little begging wouldn't hurt either, I added on in my thoughts.

Dangerous was ready to go when I pulled up to her house. We chuckled and listened to music the entire ride. I mean we were both just in great spirits. I knew I didn't want to ruin the moment by discussing club joining when I already knew her response would be no, so I waited. The music kept my mind from jumping all over the place. The bottom line is I needed a quality person to help me and have my back in this club. That's all I keep thinking now seated in Stacy's Cafe, a newly opened Black owned brunch spot in downtown Nashville.

"Hello my name is Christopher and I'll be you guys server today, may I start you off with any drinks?" I asked for a water with lemon. "I'll take a coffee," Dangerous answered. "Let me go get your drinks and give you ladies a few minutes to look over the menu," Christopher said while ushering away from the table. "He is nice," Dangerous said. "He is, and you know it's hard to find the right people to get the job done most times, but I believe you are the right person for the job!" I blurted out. "Girl what the fuck are you talking about," Dangerous laughed out loud. "Hear me out, I want to do things by the book with this club. This is an opportunity for us to show how a club is supposed to be run. I need your wisdom and knowledge in order for me to be successful. I believe since we are starting entirely from scratch, minus the By-Laws that are already in place, that we can prototype how we want our club ran and ensure any newcomers are well trained. We can continue to uphold the standards that we set now with all incoming probates. I know you don't like doing things the wrong way, but this is an opportunity for you to give some new perspective, some insight and do it the right way as you like to say. I need you to be my partner on The Set. If you join the club I would really like you to sit as the Sergeant At Arms position. I love the way you are keen and observant when we are out on The Set. Will you please help me get this chapter together?" I asked with a straight face. I was so sincere.

"You are serious?" Dangerous asked me. "Yes, please let's do this." I declared, thinking to myself, now here comes the begging part. I continued, "I need you to have my back. Preacher Man not going to do nothing if some shit goes down. He'll be barely riding that old ass Fatboy pretty soon shit," I laughed out loud holding my stomach on that one. Dangerous laughed as well. She knew I wasn't lying and truth be told she really knew I needed some help. "Yes, I will join Moon Dance Riders MC and help you," Dangerous responded after about three minutes of silence. Those three minutes felt like forever though. "Like damn! Say something." I said. After she finally responded, "Oh it's on now, I'm hot and excited now." I told her as we laughed and finished ordering food.

She made the fifth person and now it was time to get supported from the already established Motorcycle Set and make a name for ourselves, respectively. It was about a week later when I called an emergency meeting with the club. I shared with them the annual Set calendar. I marked off every party over the next twelve months that we would attend. If we all couldn't attend, at least two of us would represent our club by going out and supporting. I made it my business to make sure we would be seen, even if we were in soft colors. Seen and not heard, but seen doing club business in a professional manner. "We will start in January and work the calendar weekend by weekend. If no one can make it outside to represent and support due to personal or work related issues, then I will make sure I fill in for that weekend to represent us."

In the middle of the year, our secretary decided she wanted to invest in establishing us a clubhouse. She has some savings that she wanted to put up as long as she got it right back. We called a meeting to discuss possible locations and work shift possibilities to man the club house if we were to get one. This was a big feat to take on, but of course I was down. All the extra money I had after maintaining my household I put directly towards helping establishing our new Moon Dance home. It took us about six months for us to find our location, lock it down financially, begin repairs, and designing the leased space how we wanted our clubhouse to look. I knocked down a wall that we didn't think was needed in the new location to create a more open space for seating. It was a lease, but the owner was more than accommodating for us. My name was on the building lease along with Preacher Man so I was pretty vested in the investment project. I took complete ownership in this endeavor. It got serious when I started signing paperwork with my government name. The blood sweat and tears was going to pay off, I was thinking, as we prepared for opening night for The Moon Dance Riders MC of Nashville, Tennessee.

Twelve months later it was the big day! My club members and I had been out supporting every club we could throughout the year whilst also privately building our clubhouse. I had passed out over five thousand flyers, I ordered the local DJ for our entertainment, and I am cooking for the night of the grand opening. I was nervous because I didn't know if people would actually come out and support. I'm actually always nervous and scared no-one will come to a party that I throw. It goes way back when I was in elementary school and my mother threw me a Halloween party. She decorated the house, I told my classmates about the party, but that Friday before the weekend of Halloween, I forgot to give my classmates the invitations my mother bought for my classroom. We had so much food and snacks, music and a complete Halloween ambience. Not a fucking soul showed up. After about an hour, my mother told me, "go round up some of your friends from around here." I ended up going outside rounding up a few of my neighborhood buddies to come over and eat with me. It was pretty sad. Anyway, that fucked me up! I got PTSD from it, I always think my parties are going to be a flop. Anyway, back to our big night.

I was Frying fish and chicken. Preacher Man was at the door collecting money and passing out wristbands. The DJ had it jumping from the parking lot to the inside of our humble abode. Can you believe, The Set showed up and showed out! We had a great grand opening and at the end of the night, there were many people telling me what a great job we had done as brandishing as the newest club on The Set. Even though the club had over thirty years of history, it was new to Nashville. I was proud. Overjoyed.

I couldn't help but think of Mona. I wish she was here to see how far I came from the Black Calvary to being the Vice President and running an actual MC clubhouse. I would have for sure asked her to start a chapter where she had moved to in Texas. I pulled up some pictures of us on my phone and instantly shed tears. I missed my friend. Reaching over to grab the last tissue in the tissue box, blowing my nose I notice a text message on my phone screen. The Forwarded Text Reads: "It has came down from the top that females can't hold President or Vice President positions of coed clubs. Remy will have to step down as Vice President and a male needs to be appointed. Remy can be the Public Relations Officer (PRO). The main function of the Club PRO is to communicate with the general public on behalf of the Club, presenting a positive image of the Club and Cumann Lúthchleas Gael in the local community and beyond. Therefore, the PRO holds one of the most important officer positions in the Club. Tell her don't be upset, it's nothing personal." Outlaw Sgt. @ Arms Paco. I immediately called Preacher Man. "If it's it not one thing it's another fucking thing!" I cried into the phone. We can't do anything about the rules and regulations set forth by our dominants," He proclaimed to me. "I'm going to bed Preacher, I'm going to bed prez. Good night." I exhaustedly grunted. "Good night, keep your chin up Remy you are doing a great job!" Preacher hung up.

Just as I was about to call it a night Dangerous called. "Hey Remy, I just wanted to let you know that Lyf just sent me a text discussing your coke escapade in New Orleans. She said word got back that I said they kept giving you coke to snort and that's why you were acting all crazy. I called her, she declined my call and texted me back saying she didn't want to talk, but I better keep her name out my mouth. Now you know I'm ready to pull up over her house right?

"Why are they even still talking about that shit? I mean that was almost two years ago now!" I replied. "I knew I shouldn't have went on that damn trip with them, but I was trying to prove something. I was trying to prove that just because Lyf and I were on the verge of separating, I could be mature enough to remain in the club and maintain professionalism, we can still hang out, right I thought then." I continued, "I drowned my feelings away in liquor and coke that weekend trip. Almost burned down the kitchen with the burned bologna I tried frying." Laughingly, I returned to that wild weekend and that specific moment in my head. I was baked that weekend. Coke, shots of Remy VSOP and weed had me like a wild animal. I remember eating some potato chips and dip while I was standing next to the stove cooking the bologna when Tasha the President of Assorted Chocolates thought the house was on fire!

As I was standing there zoned out, toasted, eating chips with my hands digging all in the dip, the fried sizzling sounds and white smoke consumed the kitchen. The girls were startled out of their sleep scared thinking the rental house was on fire. Tasha came down the stairs, walked over to me with a paper towel cautiously to wipe the dip that was all over my lips, chin and nose. Man, that was some funny shit, but yeah I was going through some stuff. I am over that. I tried coke and it's not for me. I tried exctasy and it's not for me either. It amazes me that they still sitting around talking about me still. "Hey Dangerous, don't go over her house. Just let it go. We got better things to deal with like me not being the Vice

President because I am a woman. On top of that we really need to figure out the schedule rotations for all of us for the clubhouse. We need to take two days a piece a week if we are going to stick with our plan to be open seven days a week." I concluded, "Let's talk tomorrow I am mentally drained," I said as I was pushing the end button to hang up. "Alright later," Dangerous ended. I laid there with my head on the pillow and my fingers intertwined behind my head staring at the ceiling. It got very dark underneath my eyelids as I drifted away releasing my mind from everything.

A week later at our club meeting, We were organizing our club work schedule. "This is like a second job, you all have to be accountable for the days you are supposed to be at the club. You know I can't be there as much so the rotation of the days will have to include you four," Preacher Man says as we were discussing our primary job schedules amongst each other. "I will come in Sunday nights to prep the food. I will season the meats and put them in freezer bags. This way as we come in during the week, the food is pre seasoned and ready to be thawed out and fried up. I can also commit to Wednesday, Thursday and Friday nights to be at the clubhouse" I chimed in.

Dangerous chose the same days I did so we could work together. The other days were covered by the others. It was going to be tight, but this is what we signed up for as a club. So we were going to run it. The money wasn't in our account, but our secretary again put money up to get all the supplies we needed to get started, in agreement that the club would pay her back in full once we started generating income from our nights open. "All in agreement?" Preacher Man signals. "Agreed!" we all said.

It had been a month, The Set was showing up, my fish and chicken was off the chain! We set up game nights and Moon Dance started to become a regular hangout for some supporters of the club. I was having fun. I was doing what I wanted to do and it didn't matter about the VP title . I wanted to give my all no matter what because again I am a team player. The guys talked shit to me often at the clubhouse and I talked it right back to them. Life was good as the club rocked it out different days during the week.

Rod Boy from Slam Ryduz called me one day out of the blue. "First off I wanted to call and say Congratulations Remy on your clubhouse, you've came along way and I am proud of you girl! I do want to put a bug in your ear however. "It's being said that y'all are stepping on toes around here with your club being open everyday of the week. Clubs have been having bike nights on specific days for years now. Y'all are hosting bike nights on nights that belong to other clubs. I don't think you guys should be open everyday. Find an open night of the week when no other club is hosting their bike night and use that day." Rod Boy proclaimed to me. "Oh damn, we didnt even think about that. I will take it back to the club. Thank you so much for the heads up!" I said as I hung up the phone in a rush to call Preacher Man.

"Hey Preacher, I received a call from the Vice President of Slam Ryduz MC. He mentioned that the clubs on The Set that have been hosting bike nights for decades are a little grumpled that we are hosting bike nights on their days of the week." I told him. "He advised that we should pick a day of the week, maybe the day no other club is hosting their bike night and we use that as our official bike night day." excitedly I said. "Look, we are not going to keep allowing other people to dictate and run our club Remy! Us being open everyday is the same as running any other establishment. We don't need to ask permission to open our doors for business from anyone! This is our club. People have a choice where they want to go and if they choose Moon Dance as the place they want to grab a fish sandwhich and a beer, so be it!" He scoured into the phone. So with that being said, we continued to host daily open nights. We didn't call them "bike nights" per-say, but what is understood doesn't need explaining as the saying goes.

About three months later during a meeting where we were going over our finances. We discovered that indeed we had generated some revenue. It was decided that all the money that was made would go straight to the secretary immediately. I didn't understand how that would be a positive move for the club. I can see her receiving her money back in increments, but as soon as we get some money to help sustain us, she demands that she get it back. As a club, we were in a strain of the way funds were being handled. I know I didn't like it. Dangerous said "that shit shady and you know I don't do shady stuff." The secretary was Preacher Man's step daughter, so he didn't intercede. We suffered paying bills and getting food to recoup as we constantly repaid our debt to our own club member.

I found myself running to the grocery store before I had to be at the clubhouse to buy fish and chicken out of my own money because we had none to use. "I am at the clubhouse, and there isn't any food here. We open in an hour!" Dangerous disturbly said. "And its not even my day, I been down here twice now on days that no one showed up." People weren't following the schedule we set forth. Clubs were getting fed up with the disrespect we were giving. We didn't have any money as a club, but yet I was balls in to ensure we made it work.

It wasn't my day to be at the clubhouse, but once again I stopped at the grocery store, picked up a few cases of beer, some fish and chicken to cook and began preparing for any straglers that wanted to stop through. Sure enough as the grease got hot in the fry daddy, I started hearing the motorcycle engines pulling up. I was cleaning the bathroom, dumping trash, cooking, serving and talking shit as usual. Preacher Man stopped in today, but he really wasn't able to assist me with anything.

I did appreciate him being there, it was a good look even if he just sat there. Hey Remy I heard you don't like no dick!" Rudy jokingly said. "Yeah she got all that ass and sharing it with bitches! You need to let me get in there girl with your sexy ass!" LilFats chimed in. They were good and tipsy, I didn't care as long as they were buying food and drinks. I was so busy that I couldn't entertain their comical jokes, but I was taking a mental note. As the night concluded, it was packed. We were out of food and beer. We made enough money to pay the light bill at least. I didn't worry about the money I spent because this is my club and I didn't mind donating to the mission. I had about an hour left before closing up the clubhouse. "And by the way I love dick just as much as I love pussy when y'all punk asses get through bumping yo gums!" I jokingly came back to Rudy and LilFats. "Uh Un, Come here Remy! Preacher Man yelled out to me. I stepped outside with him and he grabbed my arm to pull me even further away from people that were standing outside the clubhouse smoking and chilling.

"The way you were talking in there is unacceptable in this club! You need to have more respect about yourself and uphold this club's reputation!" He goes. "Did you not hear the way those guys were talking to me? I asked him. "So what, you don't entertain that nonsense do you hear me?!" Preacher Man said as I began to turn and walk away. He yanked my vest and yelled out, "come back here, I'm talking to you!" I pulled away and he grabbed me again. The next thing I know we were in a scuffle! My face had a scar from the scuffle. Preacher Man took his pocket knife out with my vest in his hand and began cutting my center patch off of my vest! I was so embarrassed. I left immediately out of the parking lot. I never returned after that night. Dangerous had arrived late, but I heard she tore everyone a new ass after I squealed out the parking lot because none of the guys thought enough to step in and stop Preacher Man from what he was doing.

That was the end of Moon Dance for me. That night, once I had left out the parking lot I never looked back. It only took about another month or two for the club to close. People stopped going down to the clubhouse after that incident. Word travels fast and apparently most of the people were coming to support me because I came to support them, not the club. So if I wasn't in it, they didn't want to support. Oh yeah my feelings were beyond broken and hurt. The Nationals never reached out to me either. So much for them having my back. Goodbye Moon Dance Nashville Chapter. Hello to Independency.

Chapter Seven
I.N.D.E.P.E.N.D.E.N.T

A month later, with my vest cut up with several different slice marks from Preacher Man's little pocket knife he to cut my colors off, I'm boldly taking it to my seamstress. I decided to keep my vest, keep it for memory sake from my many escapades with riding and getting yonder. " Hey Maria, can you please get this sewn up for me, and its no rush this time at all." I asked her. "Oh my Remy! What happened to your vest, it looks like you got in a cat fight!" Exclaimed Maria the seamstress. "I don't even know where to start, just sew it up for me. I will come pick it up next week sometime if that'sok with you?" Maria was holding my vest in the air spinning it around like a carousel. I could see her eyes shifting from one cut to the next. "Sure, no problem. I will take care of it and call you when its ready, wild child." She answered.

Two weeks later I'm still rocking my bare vest proudly. Still supporting and riding my bike until one day I was chilling with Dangerous at the outlaw clubhouse and one of the vendors had some patches. She had one in particular patch that caught my eye because it read INDEPENDENT. I asked one of the outlaw bros if I bought that center patch would it be ok if I wore it. He said, "hell yeah," Remy you good.

As I stood waiting for the vendor to finish sewing my new center patch on my vest, I felt so proud. This was the beginning of the new version of me, no more club hopping for me, although my version of club hopping was always in terms of helping the club and bringing something valuable to the club in skills and talent. I posted my picture of my new independent patch on my social media page. Dangerous had turned her Moon Dance colors back to the club and joined me in wearing an independent patch.

After we posted our pictures standing side by side with our backs showing our new independent center patches, sure enough here comes Lyf reposting the picture and posing a question to The Set as whole asking "Is this for real? What the fuck is this all about?" Many people found it funny. Not only did I think it wasn't funny, but I slid under the comments with my own two cents. "Why is this bitch still talking shit? I mean didn't she already get knocked the fuck out last weekend yet you still fucking with me! Find you something to do with your life, Lyf." I added to the comment section. She continues with her rant, "I ain't never seen no independent patch and I'm A Real Independent!" she ended. The whole time I'm thinking about last weekend when she tried to yank on me at a clubs annual party and ended up with her head laid out on the bar counter. If I could've seen it with my own eyes.I heard different peoples version that painted a picture of her getting knocked out for trying to fuck with me in the middle of the party. She was looking for a fight and found her ass in a knot.

We were at Rebel Ryduz MC Annual party last Saturday night,

Dangerous and I. She was across the room chatting and chilling and I was on the opposite side of the room dancing and doing the same. By this time, due to the pregaming I did before the party with a few reefer joints and some shots, I was good and feeling myself. I was lit walking around dancing and enjoying the party. I left my glasses in the car and the heels I was wearing were about to have me falling across the floor any moment. "hey Remy lets go to the car and get your gym shoes and your glasses fool!" Dangerous said as she walked up to me while I was stumbling again in my stiletto Harley Davidson high heels. "Ok, let's go," I slurred.

I was following her when someone grabbed my attention from another social club and we started talking. I wasn't paying attention to my surroundings because I knew if anything popped off Dangerous was somewhere near. My blind drunk and high ass was standing right next to Lyf and I didn't even recognize her. I mean it didn't help that she had cut and colored her hair. The whole time she indeed noticed me and was looking me up and down waving her hand from behind me. Now this is from Dangerous's point of view. "You were standing there talking when I turned around to wait for you so we can continue to the car to get your shoes. While you were talking, I noticed Lyf talking to her friend behind your back and motioning up and down at your back. That's when I knew it was about to be some shit.

Lyf started poking me in my back several times to get my

attention, but when I turned around to see who the fuck was pushing me I didn't recognize who she was and was still laughing and smiling with my drunk ass. Dangerous had walked up to Lyf and I trying to diffuse the inevitable, as Lyf was now in my face asking me why I didn't speak to her. I cleared my eyes and noticed it was Lyf, my smile dropped and I immediately turned to walk away from her. Dangerous said, "she reached out to try to yank me from behind by my collar or vest back to her, like how dare you walk away from me." Dangerous again trying to diffuse the situation put her arm out to stop Lyf, "this is not the time nor place for this, she told her as to keep Lyf away from me.

Again from Dangerous's point of view, "She tried to swing on me when I put my arm out and I moved my head, she missed. Then she threw the liquor that was in her cup at my face, but I bobbed to the other side and she missed again. Then, I hit her ass with about a four to five piece combo before one of the bros tried to pick me up and carry me out the club." I had completely missed the show because when I turned to get away from Lyf, I continued to walk straight out the club to get some air and wait for Dangerous. I had no idea she was on the inside playing Mike Tyson's punch out.

Another one of the girls said she saw Lyf sprawled out on the bar top with some of her club sisters rubbing her back telling her it was going to be ok. I put these POV's together after the fact and was able to conclude that she got knocked the fuck out and yet was still fucking with me. After logging off of my social media that night feeling so angry that I could've busted a gut I decided I was going to apply even more pressure on myself to make my haters even madder.

I decided to stretch out my rides and go meet up with some of the lady riders I was seeing on social media. I mean these ladies are some rockstars on a national level and I wanted to be like them. Sometimes we have to be careful what we ask for. I noticed they were hosting all female rides and fellowshipping. I wanted to be the best so I started hitting the rode registering for all female rides. I documented my journeys going to and from the rides. I began meeting so many cool adventurous women that fascinated and inspired me.

After a few months, I decided to start my own charity ride. It would help benefit the youth I serve under my nonprofit organization for summer camp programs. I wanted a local ride where the Nashville motorcycle Set could come support the ride because it directly benefits not just children, but some of the children are children with parents on The Set. It takes a village to raise a child and I was doing my part in the village by hosting summer camp programs, but it isn't free. The first year of this fundraising effort yielding a hallowing grand total of three riders, including myself. I didn't care though because I was still going to go through with my commitment. I was grateful for those three riders that came out in the rain.

The second year of my charity ride, I collaborated with a ride that was already being held so I could already have some riders ready to go. The ride had about twenty riders. I think it was about six riders there specifically in support of my component of the ride. I was even more grateful because it was three more riders than the year before. By the fourth year of hosting my ride in Nashville I had gained national notoriety and began getting people from across the nation wanting to attend my charity ride. More people are registering from out of town to support than in town. I wonder why that is always the case it seems like. After creating a website, riding to other rides and talking about my ride on social blogs I was even more grateful for the support because people wanted to come. They were purchasing the t-shirts online and re-sharing the flyer.

I joined a few all-female ride committees nationally and brought my expertise to the table in assisting them with ensuring their rides were successes. I was really enjoying my independent motorcycling these days. I didn't have to pay any dues to a club, I didn't have any mandatory meetings and I was free to dedicate my efforts on me and my hobby as I fucking pleased.

I have done all the marketing and networking I can do and it is the weekend of my fourth annual charity ride fundraiser! This is also the commemoration of ten years of student achievement at my non profit organization. This weekend not only will we gather for a charity ride, but the event will include a red carpet award ceremony for all of the scholars that have came through my program as elementary students and graduates from high school. They are success stories and I want them to know that they can keep striving for the stars. These youth, including my own two went through my summer camp programs over the years and have grown up doing wonderful things in their lives. Some have ventured to college, others touring the world playing drums, one is a pastor now, my daughter is about to graduate from high school and my son is entering high school. It is a very joyous occasion this weekend. I want them to continue the Sankofa core values as they go further into their adulthood. As I am practicing my speech in the mirror I am startled.

"April!" my little brother yelled up the stairs at me. "April, April something is wrong with momma!" He cried out. I ran down stairs where I had my mother resting in my living room from her hospital stay. I put my bed in the living room because she could no longer climb up them. She didn't want me to have to call the fire department to put her back upstairs when she returned home from the hospital.

She was gurgling in her throat underneath her oxygen mask and I called out for her, "Momma, Momma! Can you hear me? Momma! I cried out. Her chest raised up one last deep time and collapsed into a flat surface with no movement. I thought about climbing on top of her doing CPR, but she had made the decision that she didn't want to go back to the hospital any more. They treated her like shit because she was overweight. "I'm fat and a Black woman, this is how they treat us especially in the medical field" she would say.

This last time, she was not only told she was in stage IV congestive heart failure, but she had caught COVID-19 from my little brother who frequently runs the streets, picking up any and everything due to his mental illness. I took my mother's pulse and the hospice nurse pulled up just in time. She took over and listened to my mother's heart beat. She turned and looked at me, "I'm sorry April, she is gone." She sadly said. We let her lay there and waited for them to give the official time of death.

I knew my mother wanted me to keep going with my charity ride and all of the hard work I had put into getting ready to host it. I decided not to cancel my ride after my mother transitioned. Where I should have taken time to mourn I persisted with the weekend while handling my mother's affairs.

It's the big night, I set up a silent auction, I had some live musicians, poets, a five course Caribbean cuisine meal, red carpet photography and this was just for Friday night. I went from three riders to having sold out for an accommodation for eighty riders. I went to sleep in my hotel room thinking about how proud my mother would have been watching me present each one of the scholars with their awards. They each spoke about their expereince under my program and I know she would have been all sentimental over that. I closed my eyes and let the darkness take me away.

The next day, Saturday I catered breakfast for everyone and I took them on a civil rights tour around Nashville highlighting some of the historical spots from the civil rights era. I led them on twos past Fisk University, MeHarry College, The NCAAP, several other locations that I listed on the map inside of their goody bags. but we ended up at Tennessee State University. I chose there because not only is history to be told about TSU, but being an alum about to become three time alum, I thought it would make for great photo ops.

After the ride, I partnered with one of the Harley Davidson dealerships around town and they treated us to free lunch, beers and more goody bags. We danced to the DJ who had the outside of Harley rocking. I sent for her from Dallas, Texas. She goes by the name "DJ Breezy" and she did what I paid her to do for sure. It wasn't a person with their ass in a chair! It was a joyous occasion celebrating academic achievement and student excellence with us this weekend. I awarded fifteen of my former SAC scholars with trophies and high hopes of continued success this weekend. I made some amazing supporters for my charity's mission from those who came into town. "Remy, awesome job!" Alayla's grandmother said to me as I stood waiting for the last attendee to part ways from the host hotel. "Thank you so much," I exhaustedly replied.

A week later, I attended and was awarded a certificate at a Set appreciation event for outstanding female rider. I realized again at this moment, that a person really didn't have to be in a club to be recognized on the Set for doing motorcycle things that benefitted someone other than yourself. My riding and charity work speaks for itself. All of my hard work for the past five to seven years hadn't went unnoticed. I was shocked when I found out I was going to be awarded as an independent rider on The Set. When I got the award it read Moon Dance Rider and I wasn't mad at all. I still hung it up on my wall at home. It was mine and I earned it motorcycling. Apparently, they made it while I was still in the club or someone just didn't get the memo.

"Dangerous can I come over?" I asked through the phone drunkenly. I was feeling myself tonight in more than motorcycle ways. I was ready for someone to let me rock their boat with my tongue. "Sure you can Remy, where are you now, you know you shouldn't be riding and you been drinking!" Dangerous replied. "I'm about twenty minutes away, I'm ok to ride for real. Here I come." I reiterated. I knew she was still traumatized from that time she saw me go down on my bike in front of her. I had been drinking out on the Set one night celebrating one of my brother's birthdays and had one two many shots. Speeding on the bike and I knew my suspension was fucked up on the front, yet I still was reckless. That mixed with the wet ground from where it had been raining earlier landed me with a bleeding busted head and black eye. Dangerous stayed with me most of that night making sure I didn't have a concussion. She even called off work the next day to make sure I was ok. Another time she had my back.

 "Here comes the rain," I said under my helmet as I was riding to Dangerous with every intention on eating her pussy. The lights are a blur as I'm hurriedly riding to go get me some. It seems like I'm catching every green light in my route. Tonight is definitely the night I was thinking. I pulled up and put my kickstand down. Dangerous peered from her balcony when she heard my engine. I knocked on the door and she replied, "it's open Remy, come in." I took my boots off as soon as I entered her apartment. She was sitting on the couch. I walked over to give my regular hug, but this time I didn't let go. I turned and kissed her lips while we were still hugging. "What was that Remy?" Dangerous asked me with a surprised look on her face. "I've been wanting to taste you Dangerous and I want to do it right now if thats alright with you." I softly responded to Dangerous. She took my hand and led me down the hall to the bedroom and we didn't have many more words that night for each other. It was all action. I got exactly what I came for I thought as I passed out.

"Good Morning, I said as the sun was coming through her bedroom window. Rolling over to look at me, "Good Morning

Remy, last night was great. How long have you been thinking about having sex with me?" "Honestly its been lingering for a while. I just love the way you have been here for me. I love the way you take care of me and I love your thick ass lips too. I just wanted to feel them, both sets," I said laughing. "Well we are in the thick of it now. " Do I still call you my sis now," Dangerous joked as she walked out the bedroom door butt naked.

Chapter Eight
Crossing State Lines

October 2020:

Rev. Al Sharpton demands national reckoning on hate and bigotry in light of recent tragedies in response to the recent shooting of Jacob Blake by police in Kenosha, Wisconsin, Rev. Al Sharpton has called for a national reckoning on hate and bigotry. During his speech, he criticized the growing trend of police brutality against Black individuals, citing the use of chokeholds and shooting unarmed citizens in the back. Sharpton also addressed President Trump, urging him to acknowledge the thousands of protestors demanding change just blocks away from the White House.

Sharpton's statement comes amid a wave of protests calling for racial justice across the country. Thousands gathered at the Lincoln Memorial on the 57th anniversary of Martin Luther King Jr.'s "I Have a Dream" speech to push for voting and census participation and encourage racial equality. The event aimed to build on the passion for racial justice that Dr. King summoned 57 years ago.

During the event, speakers such as Martin Luther King III and family members of individuals who were shot in encounters with the police called for change and described President Trump as the main obstacle in the fight for racial justice. The event drew attendees from across the country, including Ohio, Georgia, and Arizona, among others. I was one of the thousands of people who showed up to fight from the front lines. Being on my motorcycle has been about working hard, supporting sisterhood and passion and mostly getting wind therapy. After watching the senseless murders of Breonna Taylor, George Floyd, Ahmaud Arbery, and so many others recently has truly stirred up a fire inside of me. When Porsche Taylor, founder of Black Girls Ride made the callout for women riders across the nation to join her in fighting injustices from the front lines in Washington I knew I had to be there.

When they left from the west coast, Long Beach California headed to Washington D.C for a total of 2,700 miles at 6 a.m. on Monday, there were just four women taking part in the cross-country trek, but I joined in on the motorcycle cross country trek in Knoxville, KY. I left Nashville at 0200 and rode in the cold throughout the night to meetup with P.T. and the other women riders. We had one more female rider join in as we headed to the March on Washington on twos. Once in Washington, we met up with hundreds of other riders who all traveled from around the country. This experience is breathtaking for me I thought as I look around at thousands of people on the same steps as Dr. Martin Luther Kings, I Have A Dream speech, I'm feeling the fire inside of me real bad.

Enough is enough! Before leaving for my trip The Set in Nashville made a foot print in the fight against injustices as they prepared their own line of support in the fight for justice. I spoke at the rally and had a chance to speak about why we must take.a stand in our local communities for the news channel about Breonna Taylor and what the motorcycle movement was trying to attain by traveling to Louisville, Kentucky to meet with her parents. "We are going to march alongside Breonna Taylor's parents in their city to show our support!" I said. "I feel like we are in civil rights regression and if we don't stand up and speak now, we will be right back where we started with Jim Crow."

We marched to the Lincoln Memorial and took stage while Rev. Al. Sharpton spoke to the massive crowd of people. Many parents spoke about the tragedies they are going through from police brutality as their children lay 6 feet deep, from the hands of police. . The ladies and I made poster boards to hold up while we protest and I was holding mine up in the air when the word was given for Black Girls Ride to take the stage.

Porsche Taylor took to the microphone as we bare witness next to her as she addressed the crowd. With throttle hands in the air we represented together! I couldn't have felt more proud, especially when I saw myself on C-Span news channel while I was on the stage standing behind Porsche as she rocked the mic! I left Washington on twos and felt a sense of pride and urgency to continue doing the work that is needed in my own community. I thought long and hard on my journey back to Nashville.

My next venture was to ride across some state lines to go speak at the Black Wall Street Rally in the Greenwood district of Tulsa. I was to speak about the mission of my nonprofit organization, and what it means for us to sow into our children. Our children, our future with education being key, so they can have the opportunities that weren't afforded for many of us years ago. Now is the time to encourage our children to be the best that they can be especially given the civil unrest we are facing.

As I lay in bed thinking about my speech and how I can be most impactful with the use of my words, it dawned on me that I had never heard of Black Wall Street.The history books afforded to me when I was coming up in grade school all the way through college, never mentioned or taught me anything about the Greenwood district of Tulsa, Oklahoma. I pulled out my cell phone and begin researching. I found a particular article that read: In the early morning hours of June 1, 1921, Greenwood was looted and burned by white rioters. Governor Robertson declared martial law, and National Guard troops arrived in Tulsa. Guardsmen assisted firemen in putting out fires, took African Americans out by the hands of vigilantes and imprisoned all black Tulsans not already interned. Over 6,000 people were held at the Convention Hall and the Fairgrounds, some for as long as eight days.

Twenty-four hours after the violence erupted, it ceased. In the wake of the violence, 35 city blocks lay in charred ruins, more than

800 people were treated for injuries and contemporary reports of deaths began at 36. Historians now believe as many as 300 people may have died. In order to understand the Tulsa Race Massacre it is important to understand the complexities of the times. Dick Rowland, Sarah Page and an unknown gunman were the sparks that ignited a long smoldering fire. Jim Crow, jealousy, white supremacy, and land lust, all played roles in leading up to the destruction and loss of life on May 31, and June 1, 1921. "It don't make no damn sense how they erase history from us, put what they want in history books, stole our legacies and now shoot and kill us like dogs on the street," I told my children as they lay in the bed with me. "I just finished reading about Tulsa and I'm pretty torn up about it." I passed the phone to them to read it as well and decided to take this as a teachable moment to educate and discuss some history with them.

The following month, during my speech to the crowd in Tulsa, feeling pumped, I was fueling my fire. "I want you to understand that if we pour into our children while they are young, we can help them rise above all the challenges they are to face in our unjust times!" The crowd cheered as I passed the mic to the next speaker who happened to be the first Black Harley Davidson Mechanic. What an honor to be on the same platform as these women. I left Tulsa inspired and ready for real change to commence.

"I am ready to make some moves and bust some damn heads!" I

declared to the leader of the national organization "We Ride for Liberty, The Liberty Ride, D'Etta. She inboxed me this morning and asked me if she could have my phone number because she wanted to know how I felt about the state we are in during these times. "I saw your riding style of the past year on Facebook and I caught your message in Tulsa. I want you to use your voice next year in Tulsa to tell the attendees about this organization, the importance of our mission and why we need to take action now. I just got off the phone with the coordinator of the BWS Rally and she is thrilled for us to come speak next year about the Liberty Ride.

She goes further telling me more about the organization in which she wants me to become a member of, "Liberty riders are hitting the highway, relaying the very founding documents our nation was founded on. The Liberty Ride is an organized relay of motorcyclists who transport copies of these documents across country and finally meet up in Washington, D.C. The ride and its riders' purpose is to inspire and to remind us all of the critical importance of these essential writings and our country's foundation."

I couldn't believe I was asked to represent this organization. Joined with many other riders who connect city to city passing the baton that holds the Constitution, the Bill of Rights, the Declaration of Independence , and the Emancipation Proclamation my second trip to Black Wall Street.

It's been a whole year, a bunch of shit has happened in between. Today was the day the to mount up for another ride of purpose. I rode from Nashville, TN to Tulsa, Oklahoma. I posted on Facebook that I was taking another solo trip and asked for prayers as I hit the highways and byways on twos. One of the bros hit my line and told me to keep him posted on my travels. "I was trying to catch up and ride with you," he exclaimed. He wanted to try to ride with me, but was coming from Atlanta. I told him I would keep him posted on my gas stops and maybe we could link while out on the road. We never did link, but when I made it to Tulsa I shot him a text to let him know, "I made it." He texted back, I need to see you to discuss some stuff once you get settled in. I replied, "ok."

I was amazed at the atmosphere of the Greenwood district. The motorcycle rally was great. Thousands of motorcyclist were out. I rode my bike to the location where the vendors were set up. I set my stand up banner, table and a couple chairs up to sell some of my books. Between selling books, fellowshipping and learning about the history of Black Wall Street, I was definitely on a natural high. I was just about to call it a night from all of the festivities and prepare for the next day when my text alert went off on my phone. "WHAT HOTEL ARE YOU STAYING AT?" It was my bro from Atlanta. I responded "I AM AT THE DOUBLETREE ON THIRD STREET, WHY WHATS UP?" I asked him.

"I WANTED TO COME SEE YOU, IS THAT COOL?" He asked. "SURE ROOM 308, I'm leaving the rally now heading there!"

About ten minutes after I made it to my hotel room, there is a knock on the door. "Knock Knock, It's me." I opened the door and hugged my bro. He immediately handed me a fifth of Remy VSOP and a blunt. He said, "I am proud of you. I've been seeing you do your thang out here. I love your ambition. We caught up on some things, talked about motorcycle shit for about an hour or two. "It's getting late, let me take my ass to bed bro." I said. "Ok, he responded as he walked close to me. "See you tomorrow bro," reaching out for our goodnight hug to him. The reaching led to him grabbing my arm and slowly rubbing it all the way to my neck.

"You are beautiful and I have been wanting to get to know you a little better and spend some time with you Remy." He goes further, "I just want to make you feel good baby." He says as he is approcahing my neck with little small kisses. "What are you doing?" I mumbled. He started taking my shirt off and kissed my breasts. Oh my, I thought. Do I stop him, or slap the fuck out of him because I don't play this shit! I am not a hoe I'm thinking as he now has my nipple out of my bra and in his mouth. Fuck it, I let my body drift comfortably into his arms. It did feel good.

He ate my pussy like it was a Georgia peach, I sucked his dick like it was going out of style!

The next morning I feel something under the cover nudging me, then I hear "can I have some more?" he asks softly. "Nope, she is wore out! I don't get dick often and then you beat it up all damn night long. Boy you better go somewhere and sit down!" I said. He laughs, "ok, ok, let me get my ass up then. My club will be out on the strip today so I will see you later." As we hug and I close my hotel door I ask, "do I call you bro still?" We both laughed as the door closed.

Later that day, after I killed it on the stage with my rendition of what The Liberty Ride is and its mission, a few of my motorcycle friends and I went and had dinner together. We fellowshipped and discussed plans for the future. The time was beyond amazing and well needed for all of us. We get so caught up in our busy lives. It's nice to reconnect when we meet up for these rally's. I left Tulsa feeling full in more than one way if you picking up what I'm putting down.

A month later, I was invited to help one of my business associates from The Set in Nashville, Dixie, with her motorcycle entertainment business. She needed some help with hosting the lady riders she would be recording for her reality motorcycle tv streaming series. "Can you help me with cooking and possibly riding along side some of the women and helping me record them?" You know I don't ride so it will be pretty cool if you could capture some footage of them riding while you are next to them," she explains. "You can stay with me in my room when you come, I have the master suite to myself." She finished. I jumped on the opportunity. "I will be down there to help you, no problem Dixie!" I told her as I jumped out the bed. They were already there. I was about twelve hours away, but I was going. I got dressed and hit the slab. I should at least check my oil, I thought to myself as I walked up to my bike. I was so excited and I knew I needed to get there. I'll get an oil change when I get back, as I cranked up my baby and peeled out destined for Galveston, Texas.

I was a riding son of a gun. All throttle, gas and go stops. Dixie was alone at the house when I finally made it late that afternoon. She heard me circling the area looking for the correct house when she flagged me down. "Hey Remy, glad you made it safely. You can pull your bike into the garage right here," she pointed to a garage that already had about five bikes parked in it. "The ladies went down to the beach." She alerted me. "Follow me and I will show you around," Dixie led the way. I helped with the cooking and the filming while the ladies took to the coastline on twos. It was cool, Galveston was lit. This rally was bigger than the Black Wall Street rally for sure. I had a ball on this last minute trip.

The night in the room with Dixie was a night for the books. Not only did I assist with cooking and other small details she needed. I decided to caress Dixie as I lay in bed next to her. I was scared as hell, my heart was beating fast, but I wanted to touch her and I did. All she could do was tell me to stop, right? I thought. I went for it and we sucked and grinded on each others bodies slowly until the sun came up. The sounds that came out of that room! I was surprised that none of the crew heard us. I didn't know she had been crushing on me. I must admit I have flirted several times at her, but she never acted like she noticed. "I noticed, Remy." She explained to me and I'm glad you made a move." I had no idea she would be game for fucking me.

We actually brought our night of lust back to Nashville, TN after Galveston. We tried a relationship that ended after a fucking month. What a joke. It was a complete shamble. Dangerous was hurt and disgusted that I would do that to her, thinking we were in a relationship. Which in high sense we were. The Nashville Set knew all of the personal business. Dixie and I posted pictures of our new found love, we had some supporters, but we had more naysayers. We should have got to know each other better and kept it off social media. Maybe it would've went further than a month. It was fun while it was fun, until she was slapping eggs out my hand while I was cooking them. Dangerous had many close people who felt I fucked over her, so they dissed me too. It wasn't fun for me for a little while after that. My positive attributes in motorcycling were being tarnished by my personal endeavors and I didn't like it.

I had to get back to motorcycling for my purpose and get the naysayers out of the business. I hunkered back down and got back focused on my personal goals. I stayed off social media for a while and kept my head in the books. Another year had passed.

After finishing research and completing my doctoral degree I decided to take my newly published books on the rode. I packed up my bike and headed to Jacksonville, Florida where I spoke again about resilience and never giving up on yourself. The event had over five hundred lady riders! I signed autographs and took pictures with so many women riders! After Jacksonville, I rode to Huntsville, Alabama, and was about to head to New Orleans completing my self-marketed book tour. I had my books, my stand up banner packed down on my bike, and I hit the nation talking and sharing my books. I shared my story with the world in my book "Soldier From Birth." The best revenge is success. I was on the hunt for success and revenge, but the revenge was for myself and all of my mistakes. On the way to New Orleans, my tire blew out remember? So I didn't make it. I had to handle the person responsible for that too. I hate when people try to get over on me. Maybe the guy at the tire shop didn't fuck me over on purpose, maybe I over reacted. I was thinking how I beat that mother fucker up last week about that damn tire as I was journaling and sitting at my desk in my bedroom. I wasn't looking back anymore in the past or at trying to be anything but better for myself and my community.

I no longer care about the mediocrity, the drama and gossip that poured from the local Set. I am on a mission to cross state lines and leave a legacy behind. Motorcycling is a very dangerous lifestyle, any day could be the last. Leaving a positive legacy, an impactful one is what I am committed to. I learned on my journey from the birth of my motorcycle life until now that personal business needs to stay personal. Communication is key. Colors don't make you a person or provide personality. Being in a club doesn't either.

I sat journaling: love yourself first, value and respect your self. What you do for your community and with your platform from motorcycling is what is going to make you legendary. With this realization, I started to invest my time and energy into projects that would benefit my community. From organizing charity rides to volunteering at local shelters, I found that giving back was the best way to leave a positive impact. It wasn't just about the thrill of riding anymore, but about using my passion to make a difference.

As I prepare to embark on my next journey, I am grateful for the lessons I've learned along the way. I know that the road ahead won't be easy, but I am confident in myself and my ability to make a difference. And that, to me, is what truly matters.

www.ingramcontent.com/pod-product-compliance
Lightning Source LLC
Chambersburg PA
CBHW021719190726
48289CB00008B/2607